My dear friends, Bꜰ
unique way of storytꜰ
wind of an adventure while planting seeds of hope and
encouragement in your heart. If you feel burned out and
weary, this book will definitely lift your spirits! And for
those who feel strong, this book will make you contem-
plate great truths from God's heart.

—Frank Famadas

Minister, Prophet, and Consultant

President, Harvard Club of Puerto Rico

I count it a privilege to say some words on the behalf of Buck
and Rica Basel, whom I have known for many years now,
both as a friend and pastor. They are both "kingdom troop-
ers" whose lives are testimonies of the "here I am" spirit.

I have seen them weather storms, both in the physi-
cal and spiritual, press on when all hope seemed lost, and
maintain a testimony of trusting God through it all. They
are modern-day bond-slaves whose love for their Lord is an
inspiration to many.

—Cory Casterton

Pastor, Abundant Life Fellowship

Isla Verde, Puerto Rico

Missionaries are a strange breed of individuals—tough,
industrious, creative, compassionate, tolerant, adventur-
ous—I could go on. Most people are slightly intimidated
by missionaries because they feel like they will be required
to fly a plane to a bush airstrip or pilot a ship into hur-
ricane-swept waters to deliver food and medical supplies.
Some people enjoy missionaries telling their stories and
adventures but they never want to be included in the chap-
ter content. Buck and Rica will provoke people to leave
the safe waters and venture deep in God, to take risks and
truly live!

Buck and Rica love God and their lives are surrendered
to make a difference in a world of pain and suffering. They

are tough, creative, and so forth...you will be gripped by
their novel and stirred in your pursuit of God.

—Dr. Leon van Rooyen
Global Ministries and Relief
Tampa, Florida

Rica is a wonderful woman, friend, counselor, and above
all, mother. She knows exactly when to speak the right
words and offer a word of wisdom from the Bible. I heart-
ily recommend *Through the Tempest* and know that it will
encourage others as she has encouraged me.

—Randy Freeman

Rica has an influential voice within the ecumenical com-
munity of Puerto Rico. Her mental toughness and tenac-
ity are matched by her dependability and commitment to
issues affecting the church in particular and the commu-
nity at large. It is a pleasure to endorse *Through the Tempest,* her first book.

—Michael A. Smith
Senior Pastor
Isla Verde Baptist Church

THROUGH THE TEMPEST

RICA AND CHARLES BASEL

CREATION
HOUSE
A STRANG COMPANY

THROUGH THE TEMPEST by Rica and Charles Basel
Published by Creation House
A Strang Company
600 Rinehart Road
Lake Mary, Florida 32746
www.creationhouse.com

Cover design by Terry Clifton

Library of Congress Control Number: 2005924889
International Standard Book Number: 1-59185-817-8

05 06 07 08 09— 987654321
Printed in the United States of America

Blessing to Joel

Capt. Buck 'Rica Basel

So Good to see you again.

We dedicate this book to our daughter Ann.
You stood with us during those
long lonely months while writing this book.
Thanks for believing in us and helping
us to realize our dream.
Thanks for reading the full manuscript and
making corrections.
We love you very much.

ACKNOWLEDGMENTS

We wish to thank:

Athlene Nathan Mills
You made it possible for this book to be published.

George McKnight and Delores Bland
You have always been there for us.

Evangelist Randy and Pastor Maidalys Freeman
For your never-ending encouragement.

CONTENTS

THE STORM

Debby

The storm was terrible, the worst hurricane in a very long time. It took everyone by surprise and swept through the small Windward Islands of the lower Caribbean with such force that it destroyed almost everything in its path. Many homes were damaged beyond repair, and water was everywhere. Splintered wood, broken glass, and garbage were tossed together in heaps. People staggered about with tears running down their cheeks. Frantically they looked for loved ones, not knowing if they were dead or alive.

Overwhelmed by the desperate situation, my heart cried, *what do I do?*

The pain was so great that it made me want to cry. Yet, I held my composure. In spite of all the loss, I could sense great calm among the sad faces.

I saw a small girl standing alone a short distance from me. About five or six years old, she seemed unaware of what had just happened. I stood frozen, looking at her and wondering where her parents were, if they were alive or dead. For a moment

I wanted to turn and walk away, but the sadness in her eyes stopped me cold. I walked slowly toward her, and her eyes never left me. Such sadness, such pain seemed almost too much for one so small. I reached out and took her hand. It was so cold.

"Have you seen my mommy?" she asked.

Her words were barely a whisper. It took all the strength I could muster to hold back the tears. With a shaking voice, I replied, "Who is your mother? Where did you last see her?"

Without answering, she continued, "I want my mommy."

I reached down, picked her up in my arms, and held her cold body close to mine. She laid her head on my shoulder, and her tense little body relaxed. My mind raced frantically as I looked for a dry place to lay my precious bundle. As debris floated past, I felt nauseous. I told myself that this was not the time to be sick. Torn bodies, broken glass, and heaps of wood and steel were everywhere. *Where can I find a place to put this little girl in this wet, muddy swamp?*

Suddenly, as if out of nowhere, I saw a small bamboo shack in the distance! I could hardly believe my eyes. I whispered a prayer of thanks and started toward the shack. The question never left my mind. *Where is her mother? Will I be able to find her? Even if I do, will she be alive?* Inside the shack, I looked around for something dry. In the corner stood a plastic bag with some old clothes, enough to make a little bed. By this time my little bundle was fast asleep. I whispered another prayer as I laid her down.

Taking one last look at the child, I went to the opening of the shack, only to find the scene outside hadn't changed. I ventured again into the destruction and ruin, hoping to find someone else I could help. Just when I was about to give up, I heard a faint sound coming from behind me. Not knowing what to expect, I turned around to see a woman struggling to get to her feet. She was wet, covered with a mixture of mud and blood all over her body. I was so surprised to see her that it took me a minute or two to realize how badly she was hurt. She fainted before I could reach to her.

I wondered, *what now?* As I was asking myself what I could

2

do for her, she started to move, and my mind raced madly for some way to help her. I braced myself and took a deep breath as I reached out to take her hand. She turned slowly and looked at me. I realized she was in great pain, and I struggled to hold on to her because it took great effort for her to move. With the smell of blood so strong all around me, it was very difficult.

Who is she? How am I going to carry her? Again, I whispered a prayer.

To my surprise, she suddenly spoke. I stopped dead in my tracks, and for the first time, she looked up. The pain in her eyes almost broke my heart.

She asked, "Are we the only ones left?"

Struggling to fight back the tears, I managed to whisper, "No." A flicker of a smile crossed her face, and we started back to the shack where my little bundle, I hoped, was still sleeping. Encouraged by her new strength, I asked her name.

"My name is Vera. I have lived on this island with my family most of my life," she responded.

"Tell me about your family," I said.

"Oh," she hesitated, "we had a good life here before this. Now I don't know. What has happened to my husband and child?"

"What about your other family members?" I asked, hoping to divert her thoughts from the present situation.

"The rest of my family lives on another island," Vera solemnly answered. "I hope this storm didn't get them too."

Although I thought there was only a slim chance that the storm did not affect the neighboring islands, I tried to encourage her. "This storm might have missed them," I said.

Again, a faint smile crossed her face. She knew I was trying to make her feel better. We continued on in silence. Vera looked around nervously, hoping to find some other form of life. Sensing her concern, I tried to make small talk, hoping she would relax a bit.

"How are you feeling? Are you in much pain? Do you want to rest a while?"

"No," she replied. "I need to keep moving. Maybe I can find my husband and child before dark."

Sadness once again cast a dark shadow over me. *Will she ever find them in this pile of rubble?* She was leaning heavily on me, and without warning, I felt her body tense up. Following her gaze, I noticed a still body lying to the side of the path. We stood frozen for a moment.

"Larry . . . my husband!" she gasped.

The look on her face frightened me. She looked like she was going to pass out. As I struggled to hold on to her, she fell face-down next to the body. Here I was in the middle of nowhere, wondering what to do next. Again, I prayed for help. *What should I do? She needs to get up and move on before the darkness comes, but how? She's out cold!* The wind was getting stronger, and it looked liked it was going to rain again. I shook her gently in an effort to revive her, but she didn't move.

I was getting scared. *Is she dead? Oh no! I can't handle this!*

She wasn't dead, thank God. I took her by the shoulders and gently pulled her to her feet. She looked at me as if she was seeing me for the first time.

"He is dead," she said with much pain.

Again I struggled to keep tears from running down my face. Finding words to comfort her was the hardest thing to do. I heard myself saying, "You must try to be strong for your child."

She looked at me with huge, sad eyes and said. "What if I find my child dead?"

This was the last thing I wanted to hear. Since we had found her husband dead, the thought of not finding her child alive had never left my mind. *Will she be able to survive if she finds her child dead?* This was the question I kept asking myself over and over.

Now she stood looking at me with pleading eyes. I felt so very helpless, lost for words. *What can I say?* I had no answers, and she knew it. After a while, I managed a faint whisper, "Let's not get all upset till we know for sure what we are dealing with. Maybe you will find your child safe somewhere." I knew it was a lame effort, but it was all I could do. It was getting dark fast. We had to move on.

She took one last look at her dead husband and mumbled something I didn't understand. She was now able to walk on her own more, which made it better for me. It seemed that the thought of finding her child brought new strength to her. We moved along the path, trying to find our way back to the shack before the darkness extinguished what little light we had left. The closer we came to the shack, the more I wondered if the little girl sleeping there was her child. *Please let the child be hers*, I prayed.

Inside the shack, the girl was still asleep. I held my breath, hoping to see some kind of reaction from Vera. She took a few steps toward the sleeping child and then stopped. She seemed to be frozen where she stood, and I wondered if this could indeed be her daughter.

"Where did you find her?" she asked, her voice barely a whisper.

"Close to the pile of debris on the other side of this shack," I answered. "Is she your child?"

Before she could answer, we heard a sound. Turning around, I saw a young man standing at the entrance of the shack. He stood there wide-eyed, looking dazed. It was obvious that he was in shock. "Please come in out of the wind," I said.

He hesitated, glanced over his shoulder, and then entered the shack. Confused, he looked around for a place to sit. I realized that we were alone: this young man, two women, and a child. Though he was shaken, he could still be a threat.

I walked over to him where he sat, deep in thought, on a pile of wood. Trying to sound calm, I asked, "Did you see anyone out there?"

He turned slowly to me. "How did you find this place? I have been walking all day, hoping to find a dry place. Just when I was about to give up, I heard voices coming from this shack. It was so dark out there I was scared to death!" He extended his shaky hand to me. "My name is Gus."

"Nice to meet you, Gus. Are you hurt?"

"Not much. I'm a bit scraped up and muddy, but I'll live. I've been living in New York, and I came to visit my family a few weeks ago. Bad timing, I guess. All day I've searched for my family. I just can't believe they're all gone. The sad part is that I haven't found their bodies."

My heart went out to him as he spoke. I tried to imagine what I would do in his place. He was about twenty-five to thirty years old, in the prime of life. He had come to have a good visit with his family, and now this. His sadness was too much. We sat for a while in silence. I wondered what he would do now. *What can I say to comfort him?*

Still, it was nice to have a man near just in case. I knew other survivors were out there. Remembering the scene from this morning, I felt a shiver run through my body. *Are they all right? Will they make it through the night?* I wished I could do something.

Deep in my thoughts I had forgotten about Gus. He had made himself comfortable and was fast asleep. Vera was also sleeping. With the wind howling outside, threatening to tear down the little shack, I prayed again. I wondered what tomorrow would bring. *Will we find more people or bodies? At least, there is some peace tonight.* Making myself as comfortable as possible, I let go and relaxed for the first time since the storm had hit. I drifted off to sleep.

AT THE
CHURCH IN BOSTON

Andy

The phone wouldn't stop ringing. Where is Debby? Oh yeah. She's at that women's convention somewhere.

"Hello?"

"Pastor Andrew, this is Martha! Do you realize what time it is?"

"What? No. You just woke me up. I was up late counseling a couple last night."

"I'm sorry, Pastor, but you have a meeting with the church committee for the new carpeting in twenty-five minutes."

"What time is it?"

"Twenty-five minutes to nine."

"Um...what day?"

"Monday."

"Oh, um...give me a few minutes. OK?"

"Of course, Pastor."

"Thank you, Martha, and God bless you."

Everybody tells me I'm lost without Debby. I guess they're right. Thank God, I still have Martha. I wonder why Debby hasn't called me yet. Whenever she goes on a ministry trip, she always calls to let me know she is OK. Hmm… sometimes she leaves a message with Martha if I can't be reached. When she left Friday, she said something about going and getting some rest, working something out.

I was thinking this while I made myself a peanut-butter-and-jelly sandwich. I overslept because I was used to having Debby wake me up. The alarm must have rung until it automatically shut itself off. After I wolfed down my breakfast, I called Martha back.

"Hello, Martha, I'm on the way. Just cover for me. Oh, by the way, did Debby leave a note with you? I don't see anything here."

"Actually, no. You were at that men's meeting, so she told me she left something for you on the refrigerator, where you would see it. I'll cover for you here."

"Thanks." I hung up the phone. *I was just at the refrigerator. Her note must have become lost among all the others there.* I went back into the kitchen, and sure enough, there it was. *I've got to slow down one of these days because it is going to catch up with me. Such is the life of a pastor in the fast lane.* I took the note off the refrigerator. It was folded. *That's strange,* I thought. I started to read.

My Dearest Andy,

I tried to tell you many times how tired I was and how badly I needed to get away. Each time I tried to talk about it with you, something came up, and we never finished talking. Since you are so tied up with the church, you never found time to listen. I am afraid now that we may never get the chance to discuss it; maybe you won't even find time to read this note. But in case you do, I left for the Caribbean to find some rest, to find myself again. The past several years I have felt like I'm locked in a box. I can't take it anymore. I might not be back. Please take care of yourself.

Pray for me because right now I feel even the Lord has left me.

Debby

I unconsciously reached for the back of a kitchen chair and sat down as I read the note. To say I was in shock is an understatement. I became angry.

"How can she do something harebrained like this? We have so much to do. She is head of the women's ministry and the children's church. A general business council meets next week, and pastors from other churches are coming. She couldn't have picked a worse time! What am I going to do now? With all I have to do, now this! What is she thinking? All she had to do was come and talk to me. What's wrong with her? I'm her husband. I love her. How am I going to handle this? Where on earth is she?" I was talking out loud to myself.

I sat quietly for several minutes, and the phone rang again. It was Martha.

"Hello," I said quietly.

"Pastor, you still there? Ann from the committee—"

"Martha!" I cut in. "Did Debby tell you where the ... um ... convention was to be held?"

"Pastor, are you all right?" Martha asked.

"Oh, yes. Tell Ann and the committee to go ahead without me. Whatever they come up with is fine."

"Pastor, you always said you wanted to be involved in any decision concerning the church."

"Well, I guess it's about time I changed that," I snapped. "Did

Debby tell you where the convention was?"

"No, Pastor."

"Would you get Elder Paul on the phone for me?"

"Yes, right away. Are you all right?"

"Yeah, I'm OK. Thanks." I was shaking. *Now what am I to do? What should I tell Paul? Everything, I guess. He'll find out sooner or later anyway. What will he think? What will the whole church think?*

I made some coffee and was drinking my second cup when the phone rang. "Paul? Good. I'm sorry to bother you, but could you break away and come over here now?"

"Sure, Pastor, give me a couple minutes. Martha seems to think something is wrong. You OK?"

"Yes on both accounts. I'll tell you all about it when you get here." I read Debby's letter over again. *Why hadn't I seen this storm coming? I was too busy…for what? Oh, my Lord!*

The doorbell rang. I opened the door, and there stood our senior elder. He was not just an elder of the church, but also a man of age and wisdom, someone I greatly respected.

"Hello, Paul. Thanks for coming." Paul came in without saying a word and let me talk. "Sit down. Want something to drink? Hungry?"

"Pastor, it's nine o'clock. Perhaps a glass of water. I get the feeling I may need some."

I handed him the letter without a word and let him read it. Finally, after what seemed like hours, he finished it. He just put it down and looked at me. After a pause, he spoke. "It seems like she has some things to work out. We saw this coming."

"Who are *we?*" I almost screamed.

"Calm down," he replied sternly. "The elders. We discussed it a few weeks ago in a meeting without you."

"You had a meeting without me?"

"Actually several."

"Why didn't you tell me?"

"You wouldn't have listened, would you?"

So there it was. "No, I probably wouldn't have," I murmured.

I seemed to have gone deaf. "Paul, what am I to do?"

"She's gone!" I blurted out loud.

"That depends on you. Do you want her back? Is she worth more to you than your ministry? Are you able to change your perspective?"

"I took her for granted. Me! I've preached about this to everyone else. I don't know what I'm going to do, but I'm going to correct it. Paul, I'm not sure I know how to do it. Who will run the church?"

Paul jumped in with both feet. "First, you need to recognize that it's not your church, and you are not God! You are not the king. The elders are here to help you and work alongside you. You really don't let us do much, but now, maybe, it's time we perform our proper role. Our first action is to give you a sabbatical so you can find Debby and resolve things with her. Second, we will take over the spiritual duties until you can return."

"What about the radio and TV broadcasts and the—?" I started to object.

"The elders can handle everything. Remember, we helped you set it all up. Maybe we are not the celebrity you are as Pastor Andrew, but I believe we can manage."

"Have I really been that bad—a celebrity? It seems I don't have much choice."

"Not much. We were going to talk with you about these issues and more."

"And more! I don't think I can handle any more." After a brief silence, I quietly said, "Can you call an emergency meeting of the elders this morning?"

"Yes! I believe so. Give me a few minutes, and I'll get back to you. I'll go to my office, call the others, and cancel a couple appointments. The Lord is with you, Andrew. I truly believe He allowed this storm to come into your life for good. Take advantage of it. The Lord's peace be with you." With that, he left.

I was in shock again. *He was right. I thought I had it all together. I was the important one, a king, even a little god. Nothing happened in the church unless I did it.* I bowed my head and wept tears of repentance before my Lord. I don't know how long I cried out to God, but I felt His peace, as the apostle Paul described it in Philippians 4.

The phone rang. It was Elder Paul. "Can you be at the church in twenty minutes?"

"Sure, I'll be there. Can you brief the rest about what we discussed? It may save some time. Besides, I don't think I could go through it again."

"No problem, but make it thirty minutes then. I'll see you there." With that, he hung up. It took only five minutes to drive to the church, so I had twenty-five minutes to kill.

Before I came to the church as a pastor, I had been a missionary in the Caribbean for over ten years, flying relief cargo and church support. Since Debby had gone there now, I figured I would contact old friends and start working on my problem. I called my former boss, John—the executive director of Caribbean Christian Relief Aviation, Inc.

"Hello, John. This is Andrew. How have you been?"

"Well, praise the Lord! It's been a while. I watch you on TV. You've become quite a celebrity. What causes you to call us poor, working, humble missionaries?" His voice rang with laughter.

"Ouch! You did have to say *celebrity*, didn't you? John, I need your help."

After I briefly explained what was happening, John answered, "Andrew, I believe I understand. However, I may have even more bad news. There is a hurricane over the lower Windward Islands. It seems to have come out of nowhere, and Andrew, it's a bad one! We are getting everything ready now. We will do everything we can to find Debby, but it's going to take time."

"Can you use another pilot?"

"As a matter of fact, yes. Are you volunteering?"

"Yes, I still fly, but only a single engine in the last year. My biannual flight review is due."

"Interesting, Andrew. Do you have any turbine time?"

"Not since the navy. Why? You have something in mind?"

"Yes, I think we might help each other if you take a checkout and a new biannual. You see, a Cessna Caravan was donated to us. It's not new, but it is in good shape. We just converted it to amphibious floats to land on water, and we need someone to take it to St. Ann's. All our planes are scheduled to leave the moment the storm passes and we receive permission to land. We will send two DC-3s loaded with relief supplies along with our other planes. That leaves us one pilot short. I think you are just right. What about that megachurch where you are king? Can you just pick up and leave?"

"Ouch again! One of my elders just used those very words. He has assured me they can handle everything."

"Yes, as I remember, you had some good, godly men. I'm glad you are listening to them."

"I should have listened to them sooner. Maybe this wouldn't have happened."

"Hmm…OK, when do you think you can come here to Miami?"

"How about late tonight? My secretary will call you with the schedule."

"Great! We will be loading through the whole night, so it's not a problem. One of the guys will pick you up and bring you to where we are at the Opa-Locka airport. See you tonight."

"Thanks, John. God bless you."

"We are going to need it if it's as bad as it looks." John hung up, and it was time to leave for the church. As I drove through the traffic, my mind was on Debby.

Lord, please protect her. Somehow let her know that I love her and I'm coming. I arrived at the church, went directly to my office, and called Martha on the intercom.

"Martha, book me a flight to Miami for tonight. I don't care when, as long as it is tonight, or how much it costs, as long as it is coach."

"Pastor, are you OK?"

"No! I know I am going to be. Please take care of it. Oh, thank you, Martha! I want you to know I really appreciate you."

"Pastor, you don't need to say that."

"Yes, I do."

I sat at my desk and signed a few papers. Then I wrote my resignation. Next was my meeting with the elders. When I entered the room, all seven of them stood to their feet in an expression of honor to me. I was in shock again. I asked them to sit and began to speak.

Since Paul had told the other elders about my conversation with him earlier that morning, I began by saying that I was going to find my wife and beg her to forgive me. If I went back into pastoral ministry, I would decide it with her. I asked each one for his forgiveness and requested their prayers. I told them about the storm in the Caribbean, my flight to Florida, and my plans to fly a plane with relief supplies to St. Ann's. I didn't know when I would return. Then I handed Paul my resignation.

He received it and read it aloud. When he finished, he stopped and gave me one of his long looks. "We figured you would do this, so we already voted to not accept it," he said. "As I mentioned earlier, we decided to give you a sabbatical as long as necessary. The church will pay the expenses since you have refused a raise for several years. When you return, we can discuss any resignation plans. We will take care of this afternoon's TV-taping session, so you can go."

I just stood there. *I don't know when this day will end, but so far it has been unbelievable.*

"No," I said. "I want to do the taping. I have something special to say. Can we push it up to one o'clock?"

"I don't see why not," Paul answered. "You'd better get to makeup quickly though. You look terrible."

The taping came quickly. After the normal intro and praise music, I sat on the platform with all the elders. I did not wear robes this time, and even the musicians seemed to suspect something. When it was time for the message, I came to the mike and

14

started with a prayer, thanking the Lord for His mercy. I looked up, closed my Bible, and looked into the camera.

"I am going on a sabbatical from my pastoral responsibilities. It will be a time for much-needed rest and restoring order to some personal matters. I have put our church before everything, sometimes even before God. I have made myself the pastor, not as a servant of the Lord and His people, but as a master of this church. I beg your forgiveness. I have neglected my wife, the one person I cherish above all others on this planet. I have been so busy doing the work the Lord has given to others—the elders—that I have neglected my wife, who is so dear.

"To those of you who are leaders and pastors watching, take heed to what I am saying. The church you pastor is not yours. You may have founded it, but it belongs to the Lord Jesus Christ. You have the privilege to serve Him and His people. Don't build an edifice to yourself in the name of Christ. Ask Him what He wants and strive to do that. We build churches bigger and bigger while people die and go to hell because we haven't told them the truth about Him. People starve even in the city in which we live. How can we justify our actions before the living God? Wake up, my brothers. Time is running out.

"This is my last broadcast for some time, if ever at all. I am turning the church and all its ministries over to our elders, the finest, godly men I know. I believe that God—the Trinity—comes first, our wives and family second, and the church third. Without family, there is no church. I am committing myself to place and keep these relationships in the proper order. With our Lord's help, I will find my wife, beg her forgiveness, and only then return to the church. May God bless you!"

The cameras faded, and I took off my jacket. With tears in our eyes, my friends and I said good-bye. Finally I announced, "I have a plane to catch." And with that, I left.

3

THE SHELTER

Debby

I must have slept for quite some time. When I awoke, I heard voices outside the shack. I jumped to my feet, wondering what was happening. The rain had stopped, and the sun was trying its best to come out. At the sight of me, the people stopped talking and looked at me as if they were seeing a ghost. I guess they didn't expect to find anyone in the shack. They never thought to look inside. Everyone was talking at the same time. After a while, I found my voice.

"Do you have any food and water?" I asked. "You see, I have a small child, a badly injured lady, and a young man with me here." Before I finished speaking, I heard movement behind me. I turned and saw Gus and the child walking toward me. Vera was still asleep. The people outside looked on in surprise.

Still waiting for an answer, I asked again, "Do you have any food and water?"

"Oh, yes, we have some, but not much. We weren't able to save much. The storm came upon us so quickly. It didn't give us any notice. Come with us."

"We put together a bit of a shanty, mon, all of us together. We scraped up all the food and water we could find. Come, we share it."

I thanked them and turned around to get Vera. She was still out. I wondered if she was going to be all right. I was worried about her. I knew she was hurt, but I had no idea how badly. I made one last effort to wake her, thinking all the time that she might die. The thought of her dying made me sick. As the wave of nausea tried to overcome me, I prayed again.

Leaving Vera behind, we went with the people we had just met outside our shack. I was thankful for their sakes that I didn't feel too sick. As we walked toward their shanty, I wondered if there were others. I was about to ask this when men and women, carrying children, joined us. It was surprising to see that so many people had survived the storm. There was such excitement, with people talking and hugging, happy to see each other.

For a moment I found myself caught up in the excitement. Then the severity of the storm and its disastrous results overwhelmed me as we entered the place where we expected to find food and water. It was a mess! People were lying all around, hurt, bleeding, and making the most horrible sounds. As I stood there, looking at these people, I was afraid most of them would die before any real help could arrive. My head was spinning, and I felt like I was going to faint. The smell of blood was getting to me. I felt a hand on my shoulder; it was Gus. Then everything went black.

I opened my eyes to see a sweet little lady who was wiping my brow with a wet cloth. Her hands were so gentle. I wanted to close my eyes again and rest for a day or two. I was enjoying this thought when Gus and my little bundle joined us. I was very happy to see how well they got along. Gus was taking care of her, and she was holding on to him for dear life. She was so helpless and in need of her parents. I wondered, *Will we ever find them?* She had eaten something but still had a sad look in her eyes. Every time someone new came through the door, she looked with great expectation, hoping it would be her mother.

She came over to me and sat down. I reached out to stroke her long, black hair, hoping for a smile. She looked at me with those sad eyes, and I felt helpless all over again. I held her close to me, trying to comfort her and knowing I was a poor substitute for her mother. My mind wandered back to the shack and Vera. *Is she all right? I need to get back to her.* I started to get up, thinking about asking Gus to go back with me, but he had wandered off and was nowhere to be found. I wondered where he was. Thinking that he was out looking for family members, I decided not to add to his troubles.

Before I had a chance to do anything, Gus walked in with Vera in his arms. He had carried her all the way from the shack. Vera looked lifeless as Gus gently laid her down. I walked over to her, hoping for some sign of life. She turned her head a bit and opened her eyes.

She looked at me, and then she asked, "Could I have some water, please?"

A smile broke over my face. I was so happy; she was going to make it! I whispered a prayer of thanks. As Vera sipped her water, one of the ladies was busy making her some hot soup. It warmed my heart to see how gentle and kind these people were. I went over to Gus to thank him for taking care of Vera and the little girl. He turned to me with a worried look on his face.

"Are you all right?"

"Sure," I answered. "Why wouldn't I be?"

"You passed out," he said. "I barely caught you before you hit the ground."

Gus was an interesting guy. He always seemed to be in thought. I wanted to know more about him, but now was not the time. With so much madness all around us, it would be hard for him to relax and talk about himself. Every now and then, I saw him glance over at Vera. I found myself daydreaming. *It would sure be nice if he and Vera could hit it off, since she has lost her husband and doesn't know where her child is.* My daydreaming was short-lived, as Gus broke into my thoughts.

"Do you think she is going to be all right?"

"Who?" I asked.

"Vera," he replied.

"I don't know, Gus. She was in bad shape when I found her. I believe she needs medical help. The ladies are looking her over as if they know what they are doing. I am so very thankful because, as you have seen, I am not good with blood. Maybe we'll find a doctor before the day is out."

He looked at me with admiration in his eyes. "You are an incredible person. Who are you? Where did you come from? You have cared for Vera and the child as if they belonged to you. And me— you showed me such kindness! Yet, I don't even know your name."

Before I could respond, my little bundle was standing in front of me, demanding my attention. The sun was shining; things were starting to dry up. I felt a sense of relief. Maybe now we could try to get help for those who were badly hurt.

Again my thoughts went to Vera. She still looked helpless, not able to move on her own. Although she had eaten something and had rested, she still made no effort to get up and walk around. It was as if she had no interest in what was happening around her. I wondered if losing her husband and not finding her child might have put her in a state of shock. *What can I do to bring her out of this?*

I made my way around the shelter. Everyone, it seemed, was busy doing something. Some were gathering wood, some looking for more food and water, others still searching for loved ones. Gus was in the last group, and I hoped for his sake that he would find at least something to bring an end to his searching. Still thinking about Gus, I started walking toward an old man who was frantically going through a pile of rubble. He was apparently hoping to find some remains from his house.

He turned to me with tears streaming down his rankled face

and said, "This was my house. There is nothing left. What am I to do now?"

He was seventy-or-so years old. *How sad,* I thought. *What can he do now?* Feeling more helpless than I ever had, I struggled to find words to comfort him. I found myself saying in a calm voice, "At least you are alive and not hurt like others."

Trying to keep his emotions under control, he spoke with great effort. "As you can see, I am an old man and do not have many years left. Yet, I have to start over."

I stood there as if I was frozen, looking at him. He was right. My heart went out to him. I reached over and gave him a great big hug. He held on to me as if he was thankful to have someone near. I felt his worn body relax for a while. Then he let go of me and stepped back, wiping his eyes.

"Thank you," he said. "I needed that."

As I walked away from him, I felt that he was going to make it. Now I needed to continue my search for a doctor. However, what I was about to discover made me shiver all over.

In front of the shelter was a pile of dead bodies. People were screaming and holding on to each other for support. Their grief was almost unbearable. In this state of turmoil, I turned around to find Gus walking toward me. His face was the saddest I had seen since I met him. I ran to him. "Gus, what's the matter?" The look in his eyes stopped me.

"We found all those dead bodies," he said. "I was so hoping to find my family."

I couldn't help but notice the disappointment in his voice. Suddenly I found myself saying, "Maybe they are still alive somewhere out there. Look on the bright side. Since you didn't find their bodies, they could still be alive."

"That would be nice," he replied in a low tone, "but somehow I don't think so. I can't trust myself to think that they are out there, alone and hurt. Yet, I can't quite bring myself to believe that they are all dead."

His willingness to talk about his family gave me the chance I was waiting for, an opportunity to ask him more about himself. I started by asking, "What did you do in New York? How long have you lived there? Do you have a family there?"

"My, my," he answered. "So many questions."

I felt a bit embarrassed by his response and found myself fumbling for words. He seemed amused by this, and I turned away suddenly to where the others were already burying the dead. Before we could continue, some people from the shelter joined us and invited us to come and have something to eat. I was grateful for the interruption.

We started toward the shelter. It seemed that the severe damage from the storm was taking its toll on the people. The happy group of people I had left earlier now expressed sadness and despair. They had buried their dead, and yet so many more were missing. I went over to where Vera was lying. She was still in the same spot I had left her. Looking down at her, I hoped to find a doctor before the day was over. I reached down and stroked her forehead. She groaned, and with great difficulty, managed to move a little.

Mary, one of the ladies from the shelter, said, "Don't fret yourself none, child. She had more soup and water. She gonna make it. She young, child."

I turned to Mary with a sigh of relief. "Do you really think so? She is badly hurt."

"We know she was, but she will make it, child. We have been taking good care of her."

"Thank you so very much," I whispered. I was too choked up to trust myself to say any more. Overcome with emotions, I walked past Mary to the door and ran outside, looking for a quiet place.

I found a nice spot and sat down. So much had happened since the storm, and I felt tired, overwhelmed. After a good cry, I felt much better—relaxed and at peace. *Now I can go on with whatever else is left for me to do.*

Trying to remember what was next, I sat under a tree and

watched the sun go down. I reflected on the morning and all that had taken place. I thought again of the kindness of those dear, sweet people. *How good it is to know that Vera will receive care!* I relaxed and let go of the pressure that had been building all day. The thought of being able to release my worry about Vera gave me a great sense of peace.

Yet, I still had my little bundle to worry about. I realized that she would be looking for me by this time. Then I remembered all those gracious ladies at the shelter. *They will take care of her. Still, she misses me when I am not there.* My thoughts went back to her mother again. *Will she be found?* Suddenly I found myself wondering what her mother would be like. *Am I capable of caring for her?* Lost in thought, I didn't hear Mary coming until she was standing in front of me.

"We was worried about you," she said. "You a-right?"

I jumped to my feet, not wanting to give her more reason for concern. "Sure, I'm all right."

"Great!" she exclaimed. "Let's go back to the shelter, or do you want to stay here a while longer?"

"No," I replied. "I'll come with you."

We started back to the shelter. Mary was a plump lady, probably in her middle fifties. She was very pleasant to talk to. I asked how Vera was. She was doing much better and getting stronger, Mary informed me. Before I could ask any more questions, Gus joined us.

"Hi, where have you been?" he asked with a half-smile.

"We were just visiting," I replied sweetly. "Mary was telling me how well Vera is doing. Do you think she still needs a doctor?"

"I don't know for sure," Gus replied. "Maybe we'll know more in the next few days. This is only the second day after the storm. People are still wondering what has happened. We haven't heard from the outside world yet."

"I hope we do soon," I said. "We must be running out of food and water."

"That's not for you to worry about. The men will take care of that. You have enough to worry about right now," Gus teased.

I was thankful for his light humor. It helped take some of the stress away. Gus and I were so busy talking that we didn't notice Mary had gone on ahead of us.

4

ANDY
FLIES TO FLORIDA

Andy

Paul *drove me to the* airport in silence. Finally, as he pulled up at the entrance for my flight, he grabbed me and hugged me. "You know, I've never met a man quite like you. Take care and find Debby."

"I'll give it all I've got—and thanks, Paul." I grabbed my small duffel bag and headed for the check-in. I couldn't believe how much baggage surrounded me. Most of the passengers were trying to get refunds and change their flights because of the hurricane.

An attendant asked me if I was changing my flight. I answered quickly and forcibly, "No, I have to get to Florida." My response startled her, and I apologized. I asked her if I was late. She assured me I had time since the plane was late. She promised to walk my ticket through since the counter was crowded with people going nowhere. I thanked her, and in moments I was going through security.

I was wearing jeans, something I hadn't done in years. It didn't seem to fit my image, and security was giving me the fifth degree. They questioned why I was going into a possible storm zone. I tried to explain that I was a missionary pilot and had to get to Florida to take a plane to St. Ann's. This only made things worse. All I could imagine now was missing the flight because these nitwits couldn't understand that some people are not terrorists but actually serve others. I settled down when I remembered that the attendant told me the plane was late.

Finally, I had to show them my pilot's license. I had caused so much confusion at this point that the supervisor, a small, dark woman, came over. "Sir, can I help?"

"I hope so. I am trying to get on the last flight to Florida, and I guess I got impatient with these people who are just doing their job. Forgive me."

"Excuse me, sir. Aren't you Pastor Andrew from Christian TV?" she asked.

Now I had really blown it—not only a Christian making a fuss, but *the* Pastor Andrew. *Oh my Lord! Please forgive me. I have a long row to hoe.*

"Well, yes. I'm really sorry I got excited. I thought I might miss this plane."

"Are you really going to the islands to fly relief cargo in the disaster?"

"Well, yes, and…if you watch the TV show tomorrow, you will understand the rest."

"Oh, I never miss it. But how will you be on TV if you are flying out now?"

"We taped it this afternoon. Please, may I go now? I do have a plane to catch."

"Of course, Pastor. Let him by. It's OK. God bless you, Pastor."

It seemed strange, but I cringed when she addressed me as Pastor. *From now on, I'm going to just be Andy. I was ordained when I flew missions before, but I was just Andy.*

When I got to the gate, I learned that the plane had arrived during my security bout, and passengers were boarding. For the first time, I looked at my ticket and saw that my seat was by the emergency door over the wing. *I hope the Lord isn't telling me something.*

26

The airline was new and was flying Boeing 727s—old airplanes, but still good. I tried to settle in, wondering who my rowmate would be. Only two seats were by the emergency exit, and it seemed that since people were canceling, I had the row to myself. *Thank you, Lord. I don't think I can handle people right now.* The takeoff was normal, and soon we were at thirty thousand feet in clear air. I settled back. Suddenly it hit me. Here I was, flying to the Caribbean to find Debby, who may be involved in one of the worst storms of the century. Since the phone had awakened me this morning, things had happened so quickly that I really hadn't had a minute to stop and think. Now I had hours. *What am I going to do? What if I can't find her? What if she is hurt or even killed? How would I be able to live with that?* I caught myself. *Whoa, Andy, you keep this up, and you'll end up in the nuthouse. Then you won't be able to find her or even yourself.* I tried not to think about my fears. I took a magazine and tried to read it, but I realized I was turning the pages without even reading them. I tried harder. Tears were running down my cheeks. I didn't make a sound; I couldn't because it got stuck in my throat.

"Can't they make this plane go any faster?" I blurted to the stewardess.

"I'm sorry, sir," she said, "but we are flying at over five hundred miles an hour. That is the speed air traffic control gave us, due to the other traffic."

"Oh, excuse me. Do you have a napkin? I have something in my eye," I said in a shaky voice.

"Yes, sir. Just a second." She returned with a Kleenex.

"Here you are. Do you need any help?"

"No, I'm OK."

"Well, if you need anything else, you just push that button. OK? Everything is going to be all right, you'll see."

This is crazy. I'm usually doing the encouraging. I started to think back over ten years ago when I first met Debby. I was flying missions and had gone to Boston to raise financial support

27

for Caribbean missions and to gather supplies the churches were collecting for us. I had taken one of the DC-3s. I was in one of the classrooms, giving my lecture and using the blackboard to answer questions.

Debby walked in late and sat down. I attempted to act normal and turned back to the board, only to find that I had been facing the board. The result was that I turned directly toward the audience and was looking at her. She was the most beautiful creature I had ever seen on the face of the earth. I was totally captivated, and I just stood there. I heard giggling from some girls up front, snapped out of it, and continued on, only to crush the chalk on the board. I turned to the group, mumbled some words I can't remember, and dismissed myself— not them. Later the pastor, with a smile, commented on how good my lecture was until I closed. He encouraged me to work on that.

That afternoon I was at the airport, loading the plane to get ready to leave, and a group of people from the church was helping. I noticed that they had put a box of clothing in the wrong place. It was light and soft, and heavier things would crush it. I reached in, picked it up, and turned to hand it back to the young man who was helping me. Only it was not a young man behind me. It was Debby! I reached forward and took a step, not noticing a box I had just put there myself. My foot caught on it, and down I went, crushing the box of clothes. I rolled over, and there she stood laughing. In fact, everyone was laughing, so I just joined in.

"Are you OK?"

"Yeah, only my pride is damaged, and, I guess, this box I was trying to save. I'm Andrew um...Andy."

"Yes, I know. It must take you a long time to load a plane like this."

"You mean falling and all?"

"Well, yes, something like that." Her smile was like a beam of sunlight. I was in serious trouble.

"I need some coffee. I think there is some in the terminal."

"That sounds good."

We both had coffee and talked a little about missions. I felt better because I was on home ground, discussing ministry in which I had served for several years. I didn't know it, but it was the first time she had ever had coffee, and she really didn't like it then. She later told me that if I would have explained to her how airplane engines work, she would have sat in complete rapture. When she was a girl, she believed that pilots were just a little under God, because they were able to hold big planes up in the air. I also discovered that she was ten years younger than I was. I prayed quietly that it wouldn't be a problem.

I left the next morning for Florida, flying in good weather. The DC-3 is a good plane, but it isn't fast. I arrived late in the evening, tired and hungry, and met John when I landed. He asked about the flight and all the mundane things.

"Oh, yeah, I understand you met a girl up there."

"How did you find that out so quickly?"

"A thing called a telephone."

"You know, I don't even know her name."

"Deborah."

"Wow! You don't miss a beat."

"Well, I've known her since she was a child. I guess I should remember her name. Her father is a friend of mine and the pastor of the church you were visiting. It was the first African American church in that part of Boston."

I sat down on a box of cargo, only to have it collapse. "This seems to happen every time I see her or talk about her."

"Sir, sir," interrupted the stewardess, "do you want the ham and cheese or the chicken?"

"What? It was like being awoken from a dream. Oh, excuse me," I mumbled. "The ham. Oh, a Coke, No! Make it coffee."

I didn't feel at all hungry. I realized I hadn't eaten all day since my peanut-butter breakfast. However, all I could feel was a huge knot in my stomach. I ate, but I could not even taste the food. It could have been cardboard. Maybe it was. I finished, and the stewardess took my plastic plate and cup. I returned to my thoughts. Maybe she won't bother me anymore. I returned to my reminiscing.

"Well, I guess you aren't interested since you just got here, but the Boston church just called. The relief cargo kept coming in after you left, and it seems we have another planeload," John said. "I'll ask Jack if he'll take the flight."

"Well um…Jack's got a wife…I mean…and kids. You know, I'm not busy! I know the route. I might as well go."

"I thought you were intent on going to Antigua. Before you left, you complained that your flight to Boston would put you off schedule," laughed John.

"Look, I'll go now! I'll get my flight bag."

"Hold on, hotshot. You can leave tomorrow. Take the Aero Commander. It's faster, and it will carry what they have. You've got it bad. Only one day, whew!"

I turned and left him with his idiotic smile. *He was right. I still had my dignity, well maybe.*

I left the next morning at sunup. I made a fuel stop in Virginia, got a sandwich, and took off. The weather was abnormally good, and I arrived at Boston in the late afternoon. No one was at the airport to meet me, so I called the church. The secretary answered and said that someone would be on the way. They had arranged for me to stay at a motel room near the church, and the pastor would see me in the morning at 9:00. I thanked her and asked her what her name was. "Martha," she answered. I would get to know her over the next ten years.

About twenty minutes later, while I was drinking a Coke, I saw the church van coming around the corner. I grabbed my bag and walked out to the curb. The door opened, and there Debby was, driving the van.

"I usually drive it to pick up people for church services. I wasn't busy, so here I am."

All I could think about was how to get into the van without being stupid. Finally, I was in and sitting next to her.

"Well, what do you think?"

"About what?"

"I didn't fall down or anything."

She started to laugh and almost hit a light pole. "Now I'm doing it. We could be dangerous."

She asked if I was hungry and offered to stop for dinner. "Sure," I said.

We stopped at a local restaurant and went in. It seemed that everyone knew her, and she introduced me as a missionary visiting the church. We still got stares, and she just laughed. "Oh, most of them go to the church, and almost anything I do starts rumors. They'll have us married by morning."

Without thinking, I said, "Why not?" When I realized what I had said, we both blushed. Boy, was I in trouble! We finished our meal with small talk and got up to leave. I reached for my wallet.

"No! It's mine—or at least the church's. I have an expense account for things like this. This girl is paying."

"OK. Don't let me get in the way of women's independence. I surrendered in that war."

She dropped me off at the motel. I asked, "Will I see you for breakfast?"

She laughed, "We'll see."

I went in, turned on the TV, and started the shower. I knew she was to be my wife. *But you haven't known her forty-eight hours,* I argued with myself. *What will her father say? What will my mom say?*

Oh boy! I hadn't thought of that. My mom grew up in the Old South. Knowing that I was flying through the islands, she always told me, "Don't marry one of those black girls. Remember, you're a white minister. You be careful." I never really thought much about it one way or the other. I was married to my ministry, and I really didn't think about a wife. I didn't think there would be anyone who would put up with me.

All the happenings of the day flashed before me. *Yes, I am married to ministry! No, Debby is more than that now, more than ministry. I can't minister without her. I don't want to live without her. Oh Lord,* I pleaded. *Help me.*

"Please fasten your seat belts," the intercom interrupted. "We are experiencing some turbulence."

"Oh! What? Oh, yeah." I fastened my belt. *I wish they would leave me alone and just fly the plane,* I thought. *Mom! Well, she will have to accept it. I'm forty-one. Still, there's another problem. What am I doing? I haven't even asked her. How do I even think she would be interested in a man with almost nothing? Yeah, I've got a beat-up, old piper airplane I'm fixing in my spare time, which almost never exists. I've got the clothes on my back, plus a few in the laundry. I have a credit card with a $1000 limit that I've charged almost to the max. I noticed hers was gold. I have $600 in my checking account and $1500 saved for a rainy day. Well, maybe a drizzle. I'm crazy.*

I took my shower and turned off the TV, since I had no interest in it. I couldn't get her out of my mind. I tried to sleep. I was bone tired, and I had just flown fourteen hours almost nonstop. Yet, I couldn't keep my eyes shut. I was sick— lovesick. Plato called it a grave mental disease, and I had it. I thought it might be fatal, especially if she said no.

I woke up, if that is the right word for it. I got up and shaved and had just finished getting dressed when the phone rang. It was Martha. She said that the pastor would meet me for breakfast at the motel restaurant in thirty minutes if that was OK. I assured her it was. I didn't have the nerve to ask about Debby.

I took my bag and checked out. When I flipped my card onto the desk, the clerk said that it wouldn't be necessary. The church had already taken care of it. I went into the restaurant and found a table. I figured I would have a wait, so I took out my Bible and opened it to where I had last left off. I had barely started to read when I heard, "Ahem, is this seat taken?" I looked up, and there was the pastor.

"Oh, welcome, Pastor, by all means."

"I got free a little sooner, so I just escaped and came over. We have the cargo in the church basement and can load anytime you want. Did you enjoy your dinner last night?"

"Oh, yes. Very much, thank you."

"Great! What did you have?"

"Um...you know, I can't remember."

"I didn't think you would."

"Why not? Or am I that obvious?"

"Ha...ha. Yes, you are both that obvious."

"Um...both of us?"

"Yes! That's why I got free and sent Debby on a little errand. I want to talk to you. I understand from John that you are a man of principle and will not compromise your walk with the Lord for anything. When he said that, I questioned him, as I have heard it often. But he vehemently assured me. I am concerned about my little girl. What intentions do you have toward her?"

"Um...well...um, you caught me by surprise. I have only just met her and only last night had dinner with her. I'm not quite sure, to be honest, what I am or where I am concerning her. I can tell you this: what I do see is that I have met a woman I almost thought did not exist. Granted, I just met her. I know I am beyond myself—out of my league so to speak. I had thought I would never get married. I felt that in ministry I would be totally committed to God."

"So you have already thought of marriage?"

"Well, I um...I'm not sure I have. Well, you are right in one respect. I want to get to know her better. I'll promise you this, Pastor. I will treat her with the utmost respect, and I will not intentionally hurt her in any way "

"I guess I can't ask for more than that. What do they have for breakfast here?" the pastor replied, rubbing his ample belly. At this point, Debby came bursting through the door.

"Dad, I went to the address you gave me, and it was a vacant lot. I couldn't find anything near that address."

"Show me the address. Well, no wonder. I must have transposed the numbers. It was 131st Street, not 113th Street. I'm sorry. I'll take care of it later."

Debby looked at her father, a little glint in her eyes. "Oh yes, that must be it. My errand gave you about twenty minutes here to grill Andy well done. Right?"

"What, me? No, it was just an error."

I was surprised by the give-and-take between them. Debby knew exactly what her father had done.

"OK, what's for breakfast? I'm starved."

"That's what I just said," her father cut in.

We ordered our meals, and they continued the light banter throughout breakfast. I stayed on the sidelines, afraid I might get grilled again.

Finally Debby injected, "Well, Dad, did Andy pass his test?" She spoke about me as if I was not even there.

"Well, yes," the pastor answered with a smile on his face, looking directly at her.

"Good! Then that settles it. I'm going to Florida with him tomorrow."

I was finishing my last gulp of coffee and choked on it. I started to cough. "I'm OK, I'm OK."

"When did you decide this?" her father asked, not paying any attention to my choking noises.

"Just now," she replied. "Don't worry, Dad. Uncle John and Aunt Barbara will be there. I wanted to go visit them. You know that; we talked about it. Now is a good chance, and I can save some money on airfare."

It was as if I wasn't there. I finally got myself together, but neither Debby nor her father noticed. I felt that I was off the hook— well almost.

We loaded the plane that afternoon and planned on an early morning takeoff. It would be a long flight, and I wondered if she would be all right. I decided to try and take it a little easy, but ten hours *is* ten hours. I called John to advise him of the changes, and he just laughed out loud. He then told me not to worry. Debby was used to flying. She had flown with him from her childhood. "She will just sleep most of the trip."

We took off at five o'clock sharp. We talked almost all morning and took a fuel stop and a little refreshment. In the afternoon, she napped until we had our last fuel stop. After a little food, we were gone again. We talked until it was time to land at Opa-Locka airport in Florida.

John and Barbara met us and immediately whisked Debby off to their house, leaving me to do the chores and tie down the plane. It had been a very good day, and I was very tired. I went to my apartment, which was just inside the hangar, cleaned up a bit, and crashed.

"We are preparing for landing at Miami International Airport..." the intercom began and droned on with instructions.

I adjusted my seat belt without thinking. Once again I was brought back to the harsh reality of where I was and what lay before me. A perpetual knot was lodged in my stomach. My only hope was that Debby was not in the killer storm and I could find her and beg her to forgive me.

The plane landed without any problem. My mind was still wandering, and I pulled down my hastily packed bag onto a large man behind me. After expressing my apology, we deplaned. I saw John waiting for me up the ramp.

5

THE
OTHER SHELTER

Debby

We *entered the shelter to* find that some more people had joined us. I learned that they were not all staying with us because they had their own shelter a little way from ours. I whispered a prayer. *There is no way all of us can sleep in this shelter. It is tight now, with just a few of us.* Many of the people were saying that they had not found their loved ones. Some of them were crying. One man said he believed some people were washed down river, and others were buried in landslides.

I walked away from the crowd. All this was too much for me. What a horrible way to die—a muddy grave or a watery one! Just when I was beginning to relax, the suffering was once again staring me in the face. Would it ever be over? *It's like a recurring nightmare*, I told myself. *I will soon wake up.*

I didn't have much time to wallow in my self-pity. Out of the corner of my eye, I saw the old man I had spoken with earlier. He was sitting alone, deep in thought. I wanted to go over to him and try to comfort him. *What can I say to make him feel better?* I noticed tears running down his cheeks. With a worn-out, shaky hand, he brushed them away. I found the tears running down my own cheeks, as I looked on helplessly, not knowing what to do. I walked over to him slowly.

"Hi. Would you like some coffee?" I must have startled him. He looked up suddenly.

Before he had a chance to answer, I said, "You know, I don't even know your name."

"Joe," he mumbled. "I could use a cup of coffee."

The sun was almost gone now, and dusk was slowly creeping in. Our visitors were getting ready to go back to their own shelter. After hugs and good-byes, they left. We started to settle down for the night. Since there was very little light, we made it a point to find our spots before it became really dark. I walked over to where my little bundle was already asleep. She was curled up next to my little spot. I tucked her in as best I could, and then I lay down, grateful for a place to sleep.

I woke to the smell of coffee—what a delightful smell! I was wondering what the day would bring. As I got ready to meet the others who were already up, Mary handed me a cup of coffee.

"How did you sleep?" she asked. "You looked so peaceful sleeping. I didn't have the heart to wake you."

"Thank you so much, Mary. You make this place almost bearable. I don't think I could have made it this far without you."

She looked at me with a bright smile and said, "I am only glad to be of help."

I looked at her for the first time and realized that I didn't know much about her. With all that had taken place these past days, I felt like I had taken Mary and her kindness for granted. She seemed to be everywhere, making food, serving, and always sharing a kind word. I stood there looking at her.

Then I asked, "Mary, did you lose anyone in the storm?"

She turned slowly and looked at me, and for the first time I saw sadness in her eyes. Almost in a whisper, she said, "No, my husband died a few years ago. My grown children live in the United States. They are all caught up with their own lives.

I don't ever get to see them. Once in a while, I get a letter from them. I have been living here alone these past two years. It's a miracle I survived this storm. I guess the good Lord still has work for me to do."

"What about your house? Where will you live now?" I asked with concern.

"Oh," she looked at me with a smile. "The good Lord has always taken care of me. He won't leave me now."

"Such faith," I said. "Thank you for sharing this with me."

She walked away to serve coffee to some of the men coming in from another search, I guess. It was going to be a beautiful day. I turned to look at Vera, who was sitting up and looking around as if she was just getting used to her surroundings. I whispered a prayer of thanks. *With Mary's love and care, how can she not be better? I'm sure Mary must have said a few prayers over her. That's why she was so sure Vera would make it. I wonder if she was praying for me too.*

Mary was with Vera now, making sure she was all right and fussing over her. Once again I was so very happy to see Mary taking over the responsibility to care for Vera. It was as if my prayer was answered. I was so caught up in my thoughts that I didn't see the little girl standing next to me. My little bundle, as I called her, was all cleaned up, and she was wearing a clean dress.

"You had a bath!" I said, reaching down and picking her up in my arms. She smiled at me shyly. "Do you want to come outside with me today? The sun is out, and we can look for flowers for Miss Mary. Would you like that?"

"Oh, yes," she said. "Can we go now?"

"OK, here we go."

We started for the door. I held on to her little hand, and this time it was not cold. She seemed so happy, yet I wondered when she would start asking for her mother again. I made a mental note to ask Mary if she knew anything about her. The thought of not being able to find her mother started to make me feel sick. With great difficulty, I tried to put it out of my mind. She was so helpless, so small. I wanted to protect her from more pain.

We sat for a while in the shade. She had picked a bunch of wildflowers and was holding them very carefully so she wouldn't crush them. She handed them to me and said, "This is for you."

I looked at her wide-eyed, not knowing what to say. Standing there with those flowers, with her soft, black hair blowing in the wind, she was the prettiest little girl I had seen in a long time. I reached out and took the flowers, and then I picked her up and held her close to my heart.

"Thank you," I managed to say.

She held on to me tightly, her little arms wrapped around my neck. *Is she missing her mother?* I wondered. She was so quiet that I thought she might have fallen asleep. We started back to the shelter.

I was so deep in thought that I almost didn't hear her say, "I miss my mommy. Do you think she will come back?"

I was too taken back to speak. Just when I was getting use to the idea of not having to bring up the subject, here it was in my face again. I ignored the lump in my throat and tried to sound calm. "I don't know," I answered, "but there is still time. She could be looking everywhere for you. In the meantime, you have us to care for you until she finds you."

I could feel her relax a bit. *Oh,* I thought, *that was close. At least the sadness has left her eyes, and she is not as shy. If she can just hold on a little longer until we find her mother, that will be good. Maybe, as she continues to play with the other children, she will grow to forget.*

6

ANDY ARRIVES
IN FLORIDA

Andy

"I *thought you were going to* send someone to pick me up," I challenged.

"Well I looked for someone I could spare from the loading, and it turned out to be me. How are you? You look like you've been hit by a truck or at least a small car."

"I look that bad already? I guess you got the rest of the news?" I muttered.

"Yes. Debby's father called me, and we had a long chat. It seems that he saw it coming, but he didn't expect this."

"It seems that everybody but me saw it coming. Oh, God, why didn't somebody tell me?"

"Would you have listened?"

"No! Probably not, John. I have to find her," I said in desperation.

"Yes, one thing at a time. Right now, I'll brief you on the storm and where we stand in our preparations. Then you go get some sleep. We will possibly have a big day ahead of us."

"I don't think I'll be able to sleep much."

41

"I figured something like that, so I brought you some sleeping pills. Don't worry, they are safe. I checked with the flight surgeon. It so happens that your old room is free at present, so let's pick up some dinner, and I'll take you there."

"No, it's late, and I'm really not hungry. Just take me to the room, and brief me on the way."

"OK, sounds good."

John dropped me off and headed down to the hangar. It would be a long night. I threw my bag in the corner without bothering to unpack. I didn't expect to stay very long. At the moment, the storm was running over the Windward Islands, in the lower end of the island chain just above Grenada. It was expected to do tremendous damage. All I could do was pray for the people and trust that somehow my Debby was not there.

I took two pills as directed and started to pray. I cried out to my Lord to protect Debby, and found myself sobbing on the floor. *If I drove her to escape me in a hurricane and anything happens to her, I don't think I will be able to handle it. Lord,* I cried. *You said you wouldn't try me past my strength.*

I completely broke and felt that my heart would explode. I lay there for a while, and the next thing I knew, it was morning. Bright sunlight was streaming through the window. I was awake, but my brain was still numb. John called to see if I was awake and said breakfast was ready in the hangar. The guys had it delivered since no one had slept. I dressed and hurried down the steps to the hangar.

It was good to see all my old friends again. They ribbed me about being a big-time pastor and all, but it soon settled down. They were tired from the preparations they had been making. Typical of men with a mission they believed in, they had performed two days' work in eighteen hours. All the planes were loaded and ready. They had serviced two old DC-3s heavily loaded with cargo, the Aero Commander, a 206 Cessna single-engine cargo plane, and now the Caravan floatplane. All the planes were loaded with as much as they could carry. The old DC-3s were the workhorses.

42

John introduced me to the flight instructor who was to give me the flight check and the type rating for the Caravan. We walked out to the plane. It had been a corporate plane and had been pampered since it was new. It was beautiful. The amphibious floats were added so it could land on the runway or water. This opened up the islands that did not have an airport.

I flew for an hour and a half, and the instructor said that everything was good. I passed. I wondered how because I couldn't really keep my mind on flying. It was a struggle, but I knew I had to pass it if I wanted to be of help and find Debby.

Back at the hangar, the crew refueled the caravan. The new weather report was coming in from the FAA, and it looked really bad. The storm had slowed down over the islands and was increasing in power and lasting longer than expected. The destruction would be terrible. We would not be able to leave yet. The ground crew went to catch some desperately needed sleep. Some of their wives were there to help. The waiting was the worst of all. Around two o'clock we decided to fly to Antigua, West Indies. It was north of the storm and did not receive much damage. We could take the fleet of planes and stay there until we were able to get clearance to land at St. Ann's. The faster planes— the Aero Commander and the Cessna Caravan— went ahead to prepare for the rest. We had a fuel stop in Puerto Rico and then landed at Antigua. It was eight hours in the cockpit, a full day.

The Aero Commander was carrying the ground crew. The latest weather report still wasn't good, but it was improving. We would be at Antigua another day at least. St. Ann's had not received a direct hit, but it had received enough damage that the airport would be closed until it could be cleared of debris. We refueled and got some food. We decided to just sleep in the planes wherever we could find a flat space. There weren't many such places.

I enjoyed the flying. It took my mind off Debby a few minutes at a time. I felt at home here. It made me think. *Maybe this is where I belong. Debby and I were the happiest when we flew missions after we were married.* When I looked at the unbelievable beauty of the islands today, I couldn't help but remember those first days she went with me.

After a proper visit with John and Barbara, she would go with me on my runs to the different islands. We would talk, and I totally enjoyed her company. I fell hopelessly in love with her. She was all I thought of when she wasn't with me. After one month her father called to see if she was ever going to come back. Finally I asked her father for her hand. I think I caught him off-guard. He asked when we thought we would get married, and Debby announced, "Next week, as soon as we get back to Boston." So it was. The whole church turned out. I then flew her off to a six-day honeymoon in the Bahamas before we returned to Florida. To say the least, we were very happy.

Two years later, her father had a heart attack. He retired and asked me to come and pastor the church. I felt Debby would like being back home and all, so I decided to accept it. The rest is history.

Our crew spent the next day just cooling our heels. Anytime a word came from the tower, we would all jump. Still no go. We kept in contact with John in Opa-Locka by HF radio. Everything was hurry-up and now-we-wait. Finally the tower called on the radio and said that the airport in St. Ann's was open for light traffic. It was late— about five o'clock in the afternoon— which meant landing in the dark. This isn't normally a problem. However, we didn't know if the runway lights were working. After a discussion, Jake— the leader of the flight group and pilot of one of the DC-3s— decided that we would wait until morning and get an early start.

When I finally got to sleep, I tossed and turned all night. My air mattress had a small hole, and I couldn't stop thinking about Debby. I was anxious. I knew I should trust in the Lord and be anxious for nothing. *I guess I have to practice what I've been preaching all these years.* I had no idea how much practice I was going to get.

7

VERA RECOVERS

Debby

M*ary met us at the* door, a worried look on her face.
"What's the matter?" I asked.

"It's Vera. She is getting better now and is starting to act up."

"What?" I asked with surprise.

"Well, child, she is starting to make demands on me. All of sudden, she thinks I'm her maid. Now, I don't mind getting food for her and helping her get 'round, but now she won't even do for herself. She expects me to jump every time she wants something. Please, don't get me wrong. I'm not complaining. I'm only glad to help, but it's time she gets involved and helps herself."

It saddened me to see Mary so distressed. Here she was taking care of everyone all this time, and now Vera had the nerve to treat her like this.

"Don't worry," I said to Mary. "I will handle this."

I handed the flowers to Mary, which brought a smile to her face. As she hurried to put them in water, I walked over to where Vera was sitting. Trying to control my frustration, I asked as sweetly as I could, "How are you feeling today, Vera?"

She looked up at me, a hard look in her eyes. "I don't know. Everywhere hurts!"

"Well," I asked, "do you think you could get up and walk around a bit?"

"No!" she replied sharply.

"Why are you so angry?" I probed.

"Why am I so angry?" she repeated. "Why do you think?"

Before I had a chance to respond, she went on to say, "Here I am cooped up in this place. My husband is dead, and I'm sure my child is too."

For a moment, she reminded me of a small, spoiled brat. I had to stop and collect my thoughts. *She sure wouldn't like to know what I'm thinking right now.* In a calm voice I asked, "Vera, who are you angry with?"

"With God!" she said.

I was so taken back I just stood there, too stunned to speak, and looked at her. My mind raced back to when I first met her. Hurt, dazed, and afraid, she had been covered with mud and blood, barely able to walk. When we found her dead husband, she had fainted. I was sure she wanted to die too.

My heart went out to her again. *Here is this young woman, in her prime of life between twenty-five and thirty years old. What can I say to her?* At the moment she was not even willing to listen. I felt the need to comfort her. I reached out and took her hand. She looked at me, and her eyes were a bit softer now.

"I am so sorry for all you have lost," I managed to say. "I wish there was something I could do or say to ease your pain. However, a lot of people are still missing, and others are badly hurt. We all need to work together and help in any way we can."

"So far Mary has been taking care of almost everything," I continued. "She is not as young as she used to be. Please try to be nicer to her," I pleaded. "She is not the maid around here, you know. You need to try and get up, walk around a bit. It will make you feel better."

"I will try," she answered.

That was good enough for me. I walked away, thinking that we had cleared the air. Mary would be happy to know that Vera would not be a problem anymore. I went looking for Mary to tell her the good news, only to find her and Joe deep in conversation. *What's this—Mary and Joe? Why not? This could be good for them.*

8

My First Visit to the Other Shelter

Debby

I *decided this would be a* good time to go take a look at the other shelter. Stepping out in the cool evening breeze, I looked around for Gus. Maybe he would like to go with me. I couldn't find him anywhere, so I started to walk alone in the direction of the other shelter. I had been told it was not far away, and I was thinking it should be right around the bend. *I should be able to get there and back before dark.* I was a bit scared going alone. *What if it is further than they said?*

Trying to push aside the fear I felt building, I started to sing a little song I had learned as a child. "Jesus loves the little children..." I stopped suddenly when I heard voices. I realized I was near the shelter. *That was quick,* I thought. *It took me all of ten minutes to get here. No wonder the people come to our shelter so often. It is really close by.*

The shelter was much larger than ours. It had been put together with tin roofing, wood, and whatever the people could find. Inside was a mass of people. They greeted me warmly. I recognized some of them who had visited our shelter. Some of

49

the men were sitting at a table and going over papers. One of the ladies offered me something to drink. I took some water, which was the scarcest thing on the island.

I was preparing to ask the lady next to me about outside help. As if reading my thoughts, she said, "The men are making a plan to contact outside help. It is very bad here. We are losing people every day. Just last night we lost another one. We have so many broken people who need a doctor. The few of us who are able to help are getting tired. Everyone here has lost so much. I lost my house and everything in it. Once in a while, I find a broken dish or something. I thank God that my husband and I are still alive."

As I listened to her story, I was sure I had heard it before. Trying to say something nice, I fumbled with my words. "Maybe help will come sooner than you expect. Most of the debris is gone, and things are almost dry again."

"That's true," she said, "but we are almost out of food and water."

"Look on the bright side," I said, as if there was one. She looked at me and asked, "What bright side?"

This time I was lost for words. She stood there gazing at me with a puzzled, angry look. It made me uncomfortable, and I shifted from one foot to the other, not knowing what to say. There was an awkward silence, and I felt my face getting hot and my throat dry. *Why is she angry with me? I had nothing to do with this silly storm! Here I am trying to hold on and keep from going crazy in this godforsaken place and she has the nerve to be angry with me. I don't need this!*

I was preparing to give her a large piece of my mind when some other people from the shelter joined us. Out of respect to them, I repressed my anger, but I made a mental note to get back to it as soon as possible. I was hot! *I don't know where it's coming from. I guess I have held on to pent-up emotions so long that they are about to break loose.* I decided it was time to go back to my own shelter.

The sun was slowly disappearing behind the mountain as I walked back. My mind was racing, bringing to the surface things I had tried to forget. *I came to this island to get away from all the pressure back in the States. It seemed that everything was crashing down on me. If I hadn't left, I would have surely gone out of my mind. I thought a few weeks on this beautiful island would bring some stability back to my life. Boy, was I wrong! After only two days here, this awful storm came. I didn't have time to even explore this place. I look around now, and it is like a nightmare everywhere.*

The thought of running out of food and water bothers me. That's all we need. I have listened to everyone's problems and tried to be strong. I don't know how much more I can take. Yet, can I push all this behind me and not care? I have been caring for so long that I don't know how to stop. My thoughts went to Mary and the others. *How can I turn away from them now? They need me.*

As I approached the shelter, I started to feel better. Some of the men were coming back from fishing, and they had some fine-looking fish. The events of the afternoon seemed to be slowly fading away. It was good to be back in familiar surroundings. Mary looked around with a smile on her sweet face as I came through the door.

"There you are," she said. "I was worried about you. Where did you go?"

"To visit the other shelter," I said lightly.

"You should not have gone off by yourself. We were all worried about you."

"Well, I am back, safe and sound!"

After a dinner of fresh fish, green bananas, and some other roots, we sat around talking. Almost everyone was worried about not having outside help. Joe spoke up and reminded them that only a few days had passed since the storm came through.

Gus agreed with him. Clearing his throat, he said, "This island is way out here in the middle of nowhere. Maybe the other islands went through the same thing as we did. If they did, it will take some time before they get to us."

51

Joe spoke up again. "We are not doing so bad, considering what we have gone through. We should try to hold on and stay calm until help comes. Most of our injured are doing better each day. We haven't lost one yet."

I spoke up for the first time. "We haven't lost anyone, but the other shelter is losing most of their injured. They are very worried about their food and water as well as losing more of their people. Today I went to visit them, and I was surprised by the number of injured they have. Some of them are in really bad shape. The ones who are able to help are getting tired and worn out. The people are getting desperate. They are trying to find a way to make contact with the outside. I think we should join them and help in whatever way we can."

"She is right!" Mary shouted. "We should help them instead of sitting around here and feeling sorry for ourselves."

"Hold on, Mary!" I responded sharply. "Don't be so hard on our people. Most of them have been hurt and laid up the last few days. Let's not push them too hard. They still need time to heal. I am sure that the healthy among us can manage to do what needs to be done."

We sat in silence for a while, thinking about what had just happened. I was surprised at the strong outburst from Mary, who was usually so sweet. I had always admired her gentle spirit, and. I felt bad for the way I had corrected her in front of the others. Looking at her now, sitting deep in thought, I wondered what was going through her mind. In the short time I had known her, we had become close friends. I had come to depend on her a lot and felt that she was the only one everyone could depend on. I felt the need to go over and say something nice.

Yet, as I looked at the others, I realized that we were all beginning to feel the pressure of the past few days. Vera was over to one side of the room with a sulky expression on her face. I am sure she was thinking about her child again. Gus was also in his own little world. There was Joe; he had walked away from the others to the only window in our shelter. He stood looking out into the darkness. I could imagine what was going through his mind. The others seemed unconcerned.

We decided to find our sleeping spots and settle down for the night. I lay in my little spot, nestled between the little girl and Vera. The events of the day kept going over and over in my mind. I could not get over the hardness I saw in the eyes of the woman I met at the other shelter. Vera's attitude and the harshness Mary had expressed also disturbed me. *What if we cannot make contact with the outside? Will we be able to get along with each other much longer?* I felt a new fear rising up within me. Not being able to sleep, I tossed and turned and tried to push it out of my mind. Everyone was asleep except me. *What is wrong with me?* I prayed again.

9

THE BOAT

The next day started way too early for me. It seemed everyone was up except me. There were loud voices, shouts, and
laughter. *What is the matter with everyone?* I thought. *Don't they
know what time it is?* Half-asleep and feeling the slight buzz of a
headache coming on, I didn't need this!

"What in the world is going on?" I yelled. There was no
response, and the voices were getting farther away. I decided it
was time to see what all the fuss was about. It was not a good
idea to go out there with a headache and without coffee. Someone was going to get a piece of my mind. *They have gotten on my
last nerve!* I told myself. I felt as if I was losing it.

It's this godforsaken place, I thought. *If I don't get out of here
soon, I will lose it for sure!* I was so caught up in my thoughts that
I didn't see the small boat approaching. Everyone, it seemed,
was standing at the water's edge, making as much noise as they
could. Mary came running to me, shouting and pointing to the
boat. I stood, as if unable to move. All of a sudden, the noise
didn't seem so loud.

Mary continued to shout, "Help, help is coming. Isn't that great?" She was so excited that I wanted to turn and look at her. But somehow, I couldn't take my eyes off the boat. She reached out and took my hand, pulling and tugging at me. I turned around slowly and looked at her. She was so happy.

"Yes, it's great," I whispered. I held on to her as we walked down to the water's edge to join the others. I felt like I was watching a scene from on old movie. As the boat got closer to shore, there was so much excitement. I stood back a ways as five men stepped out of the boat. They looked a bit worn out. The boats looked sturdy enough—a homemade job, with one a mast in the middle and a large sail. The men from the larger shelter seemed to be in full control. It was decided that we were all to gather over there to discuss further plans.

Not without my coffee!

I stumbled back to the shelter, hoping to find coffee and maybe clean up while the others were out. The injured lay all around, waiting for someone to give them some food. *How am I going to help them without my coffee?* I thought. Just then, Vera walked over to me and handed me a cup of coffee. I was so surprised. I hadn't even seen her over in the corner we called the kitchen.

"Vera," I said with excitement, "you are up!"

"Yes," she responded. "I thought it was time to start helping around here." Pointing to the injured, she said, "I already gave the others something to eat."

"Did you do all this by yourself?" I asked surprised.

"Well, Mary had started, and everything was almost ready. They all ran out of here, shouting something about a boat. That's when I got up and began to do my share."

"Thank you so much," I said, "Mary will be so pleased. The boat is in now. Five men came; they are over at the other shelter. We are all invited there for dinner. I guess we will learn more about what's going on." Before we could say any more, Mary burst into the shelter.

"There you are!" she said, walking toward me. She continued, not missing a breath. "Just last night we were talking about outside help. To all our surprise, here it is. It was so good to see the boat on the horizon this morning."

She was so busy talking that she didn't notice Vera standing in the corner by the fire. Vera came over to us, a cup of coffee in her hand, and handed it to Mary. With her mouth wide open in disbelief, Mary said, "You up an' about? You took care of the food?"

"Yes," Vera answered sweetly. "Everything is done. Are the others coming to eat?"

"I guess so," Mary responded. Looking at Vera wide-eyed, she continued, "Let me help."

"That's all right. You just sit and enjoy your coffee."

I think Mary was glad for the chance to get off her feet. As Vera walked away, Mary looked at me and said, "She's going to be fine."

After making sure the injured in our shelter had received care, we set off to meet with the others. I was surprised to see so many people there. I didn't remember that there were so many of them before. *Where did they all come from? Is there be another shelter close by?* Just as I was about to ask Mary, I noticed a man walking around, checking the injured. He was a bit older than the others, handsome, well built, with a friendly smile. *Great!* I thought. *They brought a doctor. This is going to be a good day!*

The men had brought some canned food and water, as well as bread. How good it was to taste bread again! After dinner we sat around as the men talked about the storm and told how they got to us. They came from the larger island. The storm had missed them, but there was lots of rain and flooding. Some homes were lost, as well as a few lives. The other islands around us had been hit as badly as we had. Workers were helping survivors on those islands to put some kind of housing together.

As I listened to the spokesman talk, I wondered where he was from. He spoke good English with a slight accent. His name was Tom, and he was a well-educated businessman. *How nice of him to come and sail on this small boat all the way out here to help us!*

The other men sat there, not saying much. They were all very tired from the voyage.

Tom continued, "We won't be able to do much now. We needed to come and assess the damage so we can have an idea of what's needed."

Gus spoke up at this point, "Does the outside world know of this storm yet?"

"Yes," Tom replied. "We got in touch with relief sources as soon as it was possible. We are expecting the United States and England to send help. But we must first send them a report of all the damage. We are very hopeful. What we need from you is a list of homes that were lost, as well as how many people are dead and still missing, and the survivors. This should keep you busy. We will have to leave in a day or so to get this report in. It will take about two days to sail back to St, Ann's."

There was no airport on this small island, and all our help would have to come by boat. I sat there, listening to all the talk. With everything we still needed to do before real help would come to this island, I couldn't help wondering how much more this tired, worn-out bunch of people could take. Before breaking up for the night, it was decided that everyone would be responsible for making a list that described their losses. It was the best way to make sure that no one would be left out.

People were moving around, saying goodnight and getting ready to leave before it got dark. I looked around for the doctor to thank him for coming. He was nowhere to be found. Still I lingered on. *He can't be too far,* I thought. I turned around to find him looking at me as if he had noticed me for the first time.

A little shy, I said, "You have been busy all night. Did you get something to eat?"

He kept looking at me. His gaze was burning into my face, and I felt uncomfortable. Confused, I asked again, "Did you have something to eat?"

He nodded his head, as if to clear his mind. Then he said, "Yes, I ate earlier."

Still looking at me, he said, "Where did you came from? I've never seen you here before."

I smiled shyly, feeling a bit awkward. "No, I am not from here. I was visiting when the storm came."

To my surprise, he smiled. "For a while there, I thought I was losing my mind," he said. "You look so much like a friend of mine. Please forgive me for staring at you."

"That's all right," I said, trying to make small talk.

Still looking at me, he held out his hand. "I'm Douglas Davenport."

"Nice to meet you," I managed to say. "It's getting late, and I must be on my way to the other shelter. Have a good night. I'll see you tomorrow." I turned around to leave, and he kept looking at me as I walked away. *What is all that?* I thought.

Mary came walking toward me, "Where were you?" she asked. "I was waiting for you to walk back. For a while there, I thought you left without me."

"No," I teased. "You know I can't get around here without you."

She gave one of her little chuckles as we walked to the door together. The others were ahead of us. I was getting so fond of Mary that it would be hard to leave this place. *It's like I belong here with them.* For the first time, I felt so happy, so free and at peace. All the stress I brought here seemed to have gone, along with the frustrations. *Going back to the life I left behind will take some doing. Yet, I know I can't stay here. I have a life back there.*

My mind went back to the handsome doctor. *What is his story? He seems to be a nice, caring person, the way he helps these sick people.*

I was still deep in thought when Mary suddenly said, "What a day! So much planning is too much for me."

"What?" I asked, taken aback.

"You know. Now we need to make a list and all that."

Then it hit me. Mary couldn't read and write. She was worried about making a list. To put her mind at ease, I volunteered to make the list for her if she would tell me what she had lost. It was starting to get dark now, but I saw a faint smile cross her face.

"Thank you so much," she said with relief.

We entered the shelter to settle down for the night. No one wanted to talk. It seemed that everyone was deep in thought. Almost as soon as we got there, people started to find their corner to sleep. It had been a long day. And with help finally here, the men felt like a load had been lifted off their shoulders. With extra food and fresh water, we could go on for at least a week. Yet, there was so much more to do. I prayed again.

10

THE DOCTOR

Debby

The sun was high the next morning when I awoke. It was going to be another beautiful day. Everyone was up and about as usual. I looked around for coffee, as people started to wander around making their list.

I didn't expect it; that's why it took me by surprise. The doctor was in our shelter, looking over our injured. I felt self-conscious. *How long has he been here? Was I still sleeping when he got here? How embarrassing!* I thought. *Why didn't someone wake me? Maybe he didn't see me. I'll try to get out of here before he notices me.*

I started toward the door to find Mary. This would be a good time to start on her list. I stepped outside, and the sun was hot on my face. I looked around for a place to sit. It was not easy to find shade in this place, since almost all the trees were blown down in the storm. I made my way to a rock that was almost shady. Sitting down, I hoped I could be safe with my thoughts here for a while.

My mind raced back to the night before. To have some help,

61

even as little as what we now had, made such a difference. The people had a sense of relief and the hope of more help coming. Before I could continue my daydreaming, Mary broke in on me.

Happy to see her, I said, "I'm ready to start on your list if you want me to."

"OK. Let's get started!"

Of course, Mary had lost her house and everything that was in it. With my pen and paper in hand, I turned to Mary. "Well," I said, "start talking."

She said, "You know, I don't need much. A little house with a bed and table, a few chairs, some dishes, a couple of sheets, two pillows, and a little stove will do me fine. I'm old, and I don't have much time left."

"What are you talking about? You are barely fifty."

"No, child," she continued, "I have lived a long life, and I am tired."

"What about me?" I stammered. "You will need another room for me when I come to visit you."

She stood there looking at me. "You really will come back to visit me?"

"Yes, I will come. You have been so good to me. You—with your quiet strength, your love and patience with the others, the way you cared for Vera and gave me strength to go on— have become very dear to me. I don't want to lose contact with you. Is that OK with you?"

She looked at me with a wide smile. "Yes, child, it is."

I reached out and gave her a big hug. I was sure I saw a tear in her soft brown eyes.

Turning away, she asked, "All done?"

I handed her the list. I had added a few things that she hadn't mentioned. She looked it over as if to say, *I know what you did.* Then, folding it over, she thanked me and walked away. I was painfully aware that the time was drawing near when I would have to go back to the States. This was something I didn't want to think about right now. Sitting on my rock in the warm sunlight, with a soft, gentle breeze cooling the air, I didn't see him until he was standing right in front of me.

"There you are," he said lightly.

I jumped to my feet, surprised to see him. "Hi, Doc. You startled me."

"You can call me Doug," he said with a smile.

"Nice to see you again." I managed to say. He still made me uncomfortable by the way he looked at me. "How is everyone in there?" I asked, trying to make small talk. "Are they going to be OK? I am truly surprised to see how well they have done, considering how badly they looked when I first saw them. I even thought some of them would die before help came. I thank you so much for coming. We are all very grateful for the sacrifice you made to come in this small boat."

Before he had a chance to respond, I continued. "Was it bad out there?"

Clearing his throat, he said, "It was pretty scary, but we knew that the people here needed our help. The good thing is that they are much better than we expected. This means we can get back sooner than we had planned."

"Great!" I said, "This will make things a lot easier for the people here."

His steady gaze was making me uneasy again. As I turned to walk away, I heard him say, "You have been quite interested in the people here. Everyone talks about how you have taken care of Vera and the little girl. Gus is very impressed with you. He thinks you held the people together when they were falling apart. Joe also talks very highly about you. So, tell me, where did you come from?"

"Why do you want to talk about me?" I asked. "I want to know about you." Before either one of us could continue, we were joined by Gus.

"Am I disturbing anything?" he asked with a bright smile.

"No," I said, glad for the interruption. "We were just shooting the breeze."

I turned and walked away, leaving the two men alone. I was thankful for the chance to escape Doug's questions. Back inside the shelter, I found Vera and Mary busy making food.

"Need some help?" I offered.

"No, go see if you can find the guys. It's almost time to eat."

"Oh, no, not that! I don't want to find any guys. You go, Vera, please. I will stay and help Mary." They both looked up at me, surprised at my tone.

"You OK?" Mary asked with concern.

"Yes," I said, a bit too quickly. She continued to look at me as though she were a mother hen.

Just then the men came in to eat. Mary and Vera started to make bowls of soup and pass them around. I decided to make myself useful by making lemonade. I was so wrapped up in what I was doing that I didn't notice Doug had come in with Gus. *What is he doing here? He is supposed to be at the other shelter.* He and Gus seemed to be deep in conversation. *What are they talking about? It's none of my business,* I thought.

I went over to where the men sat with the lemonade. Every one was thirsty, and the jug was empty in no time. Satisfied with the job I had done, I walked away to think about my life and what to do about it. I could hear the voices coming from the shelter. The tension from the last few days seemed to have lifted; everyone was hopeful. Breathing a sigh of relief, I walked on, trying to find a quiet spot to think.

My mind was a mess—confused with so many things going on at the same time. *Where do I fit in all this? My life is not here. I can't let myself become too involved. Yet there is such peace here and a sense of belonging. I want that. Everyone makes me feel so welcome, as if I am part of them.* I realized that they didn't know anything about me. *What a trusting bunch of people! However, I know the time is coming when I will have to tell them about me.* The thought of it scared me to death. *If only we could go on the way things are, but life is not that simple. For now, I will just relax and try not to think about me.*

I came to a shady spot, and thinking no one would find me there, I sat down. That thought was short-lived. No sooner had I sat down than Gus showed up.

"What are you doing here?"

"Are you following me?"

He smiled, showing perfect white teeth. *He is so handsome*, I thought, as he stood there looking at me.

"As a matter of fact, I was looking for you. You always seem to be wandering off by yourself. You seem to have quite a lot on your mind lately."

"Yes..." I said lamely. "I have a lot I need to sort out. The time for me to leave this beautiful island and go back to the rat race of the real world is getting closer," I said sadly.

"What part of the real world will you be going back to?" he asked.

"The U.S."

"Really?" he asked, looking surprised. "What part?"

"Boston," I replied, looking away. I didn't want him to see the sadness in my eyes. Yet, I knew he heard the pain in my voice.

"What are you running away from?" he asked in a gentle voice. "Do you want to talk about it?"

The tone of his voice caught me off guard. I felt the hot tears running down my cheeks, and there was nothing I could do about it. *This is it*, I thought. *No holding back now.*

I was standing with my back to him, not wanting him to see me cry. He reached over and gently turned me around to face him. I kept my eyes down, as the tears flowed down my face. I felt a bit silly for crying like a baby, but there was no way I could stop it.

He put his big strong arms around me and held me as I continued to cry. He stood there holding me, not saying a word. All the pent-up emotions, frustration, and fear seemed to have surfaced. As my tears started to slow down, I thought the others might misunderstand if they would see us like this. I drew back from him and sat down; he sat next to me.

After a while, he said, "I am sorry. If you don't want to talk about it, that's OK."

But I wanted to talk about it. *Where do I start? There's so much pain, hurt, deception. Would he understand?* I felt it was best to leave it there until next time. The hurts were still very much on the surface. I couldn't take the chance of breaking down again. *Maybe I'll feel better in the next few days.* I turned around and looked at him.

"Thank you for understanding," I said. "I would rather not talk about it right now. I need to straighten out a few things in my mind and figure out where I am going from here. I came to this island to get away, hoping to rest and be as far as possible from my problems. It sure didn't work out as I had planned. Here we are, sitting on a log on this almost destroyed island and crowded together in a shelter with people we didn't know before. Yet, even with all our problems, we can still care for each other. It's amazing how easy it is to forget about our own troubles when others are worse off than us."

"You know, I don't even know your name," he said suddenly. "We all refer to you as the stranger."

"My name is Deborah."

He looked at me with a twinkle in his eyes and said, "You look like a Deborah."

"What makes you think so?"

"It's a Bible name, and you have been a Good Samaritan."

"Well," I said, "thank you."

We got up and started back to the shelter. It was fun being with Gus. He was easy to talk to and quite understanding. I hoped that he and Vera would hit it off, that is, if he were not already spoken for. We arrived at the shelter and found everyone assembled together to make final plans for the departure of the men from the ship the next day. People were excited, talking almost on top of one another. Everyone looked up as we walked in.

"There you are," Mary said, "We are turning our lists in so the men can take them back."

"Great," I said. "Did everyone have theirs?"

"Yes, we were able to put them all together so the men won't have to wait. They are planning to leave at first light in the morning." Mary went on to say. "We are planning an early dinner so we will have plenty of time to say good-bye."

"Is there anything you want me to do?"

She stopped and took a good look at me. "Were you crying?" she asked.

Before I had a chance to answer, she said, "Your eyes look like you were crying."

I felt as if she was looking right through me, and I turned away without answering. As I turned, I bumped into Doug, almost knocking both of us over.

"Steady there," he said as he reached out a hand to catch me and break my fall. I felt so stupid standing in front of him.

Still holding onto my arm, he said, "Where are you going in such a hurry?"

"You can let go of my arm now," I said, "I'm OK. Thank you for saving me."

"Well, I don't know," he said, "you bumped into me pretty hard."

He was teasing me now, and I was in no mood to be teased. Seeing the frustration on my face, he let go of my arm. I walked over to where Mary was busy cooking. I felt I needed to say something to her. She looked up and smiled as I approached. I could always count on Mary to make me feel better.

"Mary," I said, "I am sorry I ran out on you like this. Please forgive me."

"Not a problem at all, child," she said, with a hefty laugh.

"I was just thinking that the time is coming soon when I will have to leave this place. I am not looking forward to it."

"You can stay as long as you want," Mary said.

"I know, and thank you for making me feel so much at home."

I continued, "You know, I wish I didn't have another life out there. I could easily lose myself in this place. I am so tired of big cities and large crowds. I think I have had enough of both."

"Well, look at it this way; you still have about two weeks before you will be able to leave."

"That's true," I replied, "but that doesn't make it easier for me. I think about it all the time. I will miss you all so much. I am afraid I have become very attached to you and this island. You have become a second family to me. I love you so very much."

"We love you too, child. Now look what you have gone and done. You made me cry." She turned away as she wiped tears from her eyes.

I felt it was time to leave her alone with dinner and her thoughts. As I turned to walk away, I saw Vera and Gus in conversation a little ways from the others. That was good. I wondered what they were talking about. I hoped it wasn't about me. Gus and Vera made a good-looking couple, and Vera was doing much better each day. She was not as sad, and I noticed she was spending lots of time with the little girl I had found.

My sweet little bundle, as I called her, was now known as "Princess." She was a happy little girl now, and it seemed that she didn't ask for her mommy as much as before. She spent lots of time with Vera, and I was grateful for that. We had learned that her parents were both missing from the storm and were believed to be dead. *Since Vera hasn't found her child, it would be so nice if they could get together. Vera showers her with love. I guess she is making up for the loss of her own child.*

Deep in thought, I walked outside to find Princess. She was playing happily with the other children. I stood looking at her, remembering the time I found her. She was so different now—happy—and the sadness in her eyes was gone. Her laughter rang out through the shelter as she played. How beautiful she was! *I will always remember her—her wavy black hair blowing in the wind and her dark brown eyes full of innocence. That's how I will always remember her.*

It seemed we had just eaten lunch, and it was time for dinner already. Mary and Vera were busy as usual, getting things ready. I went back inside to see if I could be of help. Mary was humming softly and looked up and smiled at me. Vera was her usual quiet self.

"What's for dinner?" I asked sweetly.

"We are having rice for a change," Mary offered, "and some more goodies."

"That's nice," I said. "Any fish? Yep! That too."

Just then, Mary looked up and said, "Doug will be joining us tonight for dinner. He and the other men are leaving early in the morning, and we will not see them again for a long time."

Mary looked closely at me, as if she hoped to find something. I began to feel embarrassed under her gaze. *Why was she looking at me this way? Had something been said about Doug and me? But what? I have made it a point to stay out of Doug's way. He made me uncomfortable, with his steady gaze. I wonder, does everyone notice the way he looks at me?*

I felt my face getting hot and turned around to escape. As I made my way toward the door, Doug and Gus were entering the shelter. I stood there, not knowing what to do next. I felt like a trapped animal.

"Hi Deb," Gus said with a smile, breaking in on my thoughts. At that everyone looked around at me. Doug had an amused look on his face. I smiled, nodded, and walked by them and out the door.

My head was spinning. I felt stupid and confused at the same time. *What is going on with me? Why does the sight of Doug make me feel so uncomfortable? How can I go in there and eat with so much going on in my head? Yet, I know I must be brave and face Doug.* Before I had a chance to think more about it, I heard footsteps behind me. Looking around, I saw Doug walking toward me. *Oh, no!* I thought. *Here he comes. He must not see me looking like this.*

"The others are waiting for you to eat." he said.

"I'm sorry," I said, trying to sound calm. "I didn't mean to hold up dinner. I just wanted to take in as much of this beautiful sunset as possible. It's not every day I get to enjoy such beauty."

"Well put," he said, looking at me with a twinkle in his warm brown eyes.

I tried to avoid his eyes. They seemed to look right through me.

"OK then, let's not keep the others waiting."

We started back to the shelter in silence. I was hoping we could get there without having to talk any more. I really didn't want to get into anything deep. After my earlier close call with Gus, I didn't want a repeat performance.

We were almost to the shelter when he said, "So, it's Deb?"

I turned and looked at him, startled by his remark. It took me a second to collect my thoughts. "It's Deborah," I said lightly.

"Oh, why does Gus call you Deb?" he teased.

I had no chance to answer.

"Time to eat," Gus greeted us.

I found a spot and sat down at the far end of the shelter, trying to avoid Doug as much as possible. Mary and Vera were sitting with some of the ladies and children, enjoying their food. The men were eating and talking about big plans to rebuild the island. They sounded excited and sure of themselves. I found myself wondering if I would see this island again. I sat there so lost in my thoughts that I didn't notice Mary standing almost in front of me.

"You didn't like my food?" she asked.

I looked down at my plate and realized that I had not touched my food. "I'm sorry, Mary. I'm just not hungry. We had a big lunch, and as you know, I am not a big eater."

She looked at me, shook her head, and walked away. I drifted back to my old life in Boston. I struggled with the thought of going back. *Does anyone miss me? All anyone knows is that I went to an island. I'm sure no one would suspect that I'm on this devastated island.* The thought occurred to me that I could have died in this storm without anyone knowing where I was. That made me shiver.

I got up to stretch my legs. The sun had gone over the mountain, and the dusk was closing in. Soon it would be too dark to go outside. The men should be going back to the other shelter. Then I remembered that only the doctor was here from the other group. *Why isn't he going back? Something is not right.* I was standing with my back to the room, looking out the window, as usual, deep in thought.

Suddenly I felt him standing behind me. I turned around and said, "Good night. Have a good and safe sail back." I continued before he had a chance to respond. "Will you be coming back?"

"Why...no," he said, teasing. "I am not leaving."

"Not leaving! What do you mean?" I burst out.

"Well, there are lots of sick people here, so everyone thinks I should stay a while and take care of them."

He stood looking at me. Again I felt uncomfortable. *Why does he make me feel this way? The way he looks at me— it's as if he is reading my thoughts.*

I said suddenly, "Won't your family miss you?"

"Nah," he said. "They are used to me being away for long periods of time."

"So, are you planning on sleeping here?"

"No, I am going back to the other shelter to sleep. They have more room there."

"Well," I said, "you'd better be going. It's getting dark."

"I'm not afraid of the dark," he said, "and besides, I have a flashlight."

I turned my attention back to the window. The darkness had almost overcome what little light was left. We stood there in silence.

Then he said, "I guess I should be going. Have a good night."

Then he was gone. I decided it was time for me to find my spot and settle down. Everyone was already in his or her spot, tucked in for the night. As I lay between Vera and Princess, I noticed that they were already asleep. *I wish I could go to sleep that quickly. Not a chance—there is too much going on in my mind at this moment for me to fall asleep.*

I lay there wondering how I was going to go through another day without telling Gus or Doug my story. *It was bad enough with just Gus, but now I have Doug to deal with. I wish he were going back with the others.*

Yet, it gave me a warm feeling to know he would be around. *What is going on with me? I haven't felt this way in a long time. Am I starting to have feelings for him? No,* I thought, *I can't let myself think this way.* As I was drifting off to sleep, I whispered a prayer again.

11

THE RAIN

Debby

I woke to the sound of rain falling on the tin rooftop. *Oh no, I* thought, *not rain! Here we were having such beautiful sunny days.* Then I thought, *but we need the rain for fresh water.* Just when I was starting to enjoy the sound of music on the rooftop, a drop of water fell right on the middle of my face. Looking up, I saw that I was in a spot to get a good bath. The water was everywhere—not dripping, but pouring through holes in the roof.

"Great!" I said, as I scrambled to my feet. "This is a great way to take a bath." Looking around I saw the others at the far side of the shelter, the only dry spot. I stumbled over to them, wiping my face.

"This is not good." Joe said. "This is way too much rain. If it doesn't stop soon, we will all be drenched."

"Oh, no!" I said, "Not again, just when things were going so well."

Gus spoke up. "Look on the bright side. We need the rain. We can all have baths as well."

He never got a chance to finish. Mary jumped in, "We could wash some of our dirty things."

"That's great," Vera said. "And how we gonna dry them?"

I decided to stay away from this one.

Gus looked over at Vera and said, "Don't worry. I will make a line inside by the fire. Things will dry in no time."

"If you say so," she mumbled.

At this point, I had my coffee. It warmed me up a bit. I looked around for Mary, but she had wandered off. Of course she couldn't go too far, I noticed her standing with her back to us, with her head bowed. She was praying.

The rain stopped suddenly, and we all breathed a sigh of relief. I looked over to where Mary was and whispered a prayer of thanks. *The sun is trying to come out, thank God. Maybe Gus won't have to string up a clothesline after all.*

People started to wander around. The guys went and collected the drinking water. We had quite a collection, which should last us for a while if we were careful. We got our dirty things and started to make an effort to clean them. As it turned out, Gus had to string out the extra line because there were not enough bushes to hang the extra clothes.

It seemed that everything was wet. Joe came in with a large amount of wood and said we needed to light another fire inside the shelter to dry things up. *What a great idea!* I thought. While Joe was starting the fire, Gus and some of the others went up on the roof to patch the holes. The sun was getting hot, and the children were outside laughing, running, playing in the mud puddles. *We will have to give them a good bath before bedtime,* I thought, smiling.

"You should smile more," Doug said. "You have a beautiful smile."

I was startled by his sudden appearance. *How long had he been standing there? The way he sneaked up on me was getting on my nerves.*

"Hi, Doug," I said, ignoring his remark, "How was it at your shelter with all the rain?"

"A few leaks and some wet things, but not as bad as I had expected."

"Well," I continued, "we had a good bit of the rain inside the shelter. I am not complaining; we needed the water. Gus and the others are up there trying to fix and mend so we will not have a repeat performance."

"In that case, I will go give them a hand," he replied. He walked off and left me standing there, staring at his back. *How sure of himself he is! He has a way of making one feel that his time cannot be wasted.* I turned around to see Mary coming toward me.

"You done washing, child?" She said in West Indian.

"Yes, I'm finished. Do you want me to help you?" I asked. "I know you are taking care of the men's clothes as well."

"No," she said. "I'm all done." She went on to say, "It won't be long now, and everything will be dry."

"As long the sun stays out," I added.

"That's right!" She said with a chuckle, as we walked into the shelter to start lunch.

With the fire burning inside, things were drying quickly. Doug had already been in to check on the injured when I saw him outside. The others from the ship had, as they had planned, made an early start back to the big island. Doug planned to spend most of his time here with us.

This is not going to be easy for me. Still, he is a good doctor, and the injured seem to have improved so much since he's been here. I am sure some of them would have died, had it not been for him and Mary's prayers. What a combination!

Pushing all this to the back of my mind, I hurried to help Mary, who was busy trying to open a coconut. I had grown accustomed to the native foods now, and I found that I liked most of them. Mary was able to make almost everything taste good. I loved the rice she made with little green peas. Sometimes she made it with some green leaves she called "callow." This was my favorite when she mixed coconut milk with it. It was so good!

The food was ready, and the men came in, looking pleased with themselves. "Well, we made sure every hole is stopped up, and the next time it rains, the water will stay outside." Joe gave a toothless grin.

Gus continued, "The doctor is not used to working with a hammer. He almost smashed his fingers." Everyone had a good laugh at that. One could see that Doug was quite out of place with this bunch. Yet he was a good sport.

They sat down to eat, still in good spirits. I sat with Mary and Vera, enjoying their company and the food. Though the conversation was jovial, everyone's mind was on the small boat sailing to the big island. *Would it get there safely? Did it get caught in the heavy downpour this morning?* There was no way of knowing. It was such a helpless feeling. Although no one spoke of it, worry was heavy in the air. All we could do now was wait and keep busy, hoping that the boat would safely arrive at its destination. I prayed again!

12

DEBORAH'S STORM

Debby

Lunch *was finished, and people* started to move around. I was getting a bit restless, so I decided to go over to the other shelter to see how the others were doing. *Since Doug is over here, I will go there. That way we will stay out of each other's way.* I slowly walked out the door, hoping that no one saw me. *Great!* I thought. *I can escape for a good long time. Mary and Vera will take care of things over here. I love walking. This is great excise for me.*

I was taking my time, lingering along the path to smell the wildflowers. I always love to smell wildflowers, so fresh and beautiful. Yet, they would not last long after they were picked in this hot sun. I continued on slowly, enjoying the sweet smell of my flowers. I was almost there. I could see the shelter up ahead. To my right, I noticed some wildflowers I had not seen before. I turned off the path to pick them.

As I stepped forward, I scraped my arm on a hidden branch. I pulled my arm back as the blood came to the surface. It was not a big cut, but it was very painful. Trying to hold on to my arm and the flowers at the same time, I struggled to get back on the path. I was beginning to feel a bit faint; the smell and sight of blood does that to me. I sat down and held on to my arm tightly, with my eyes closed. Then I must have fainted.

When I opened my eyes, Doug was bending over me with a worried look on his face. I tried to get up, but he put his hand on my shoulder and said lightly, "Lay still for a while."

"What happened?" I asked. "How did I get to this shelter? The last thing I remember I was sitting on the side of the path holding onto my arm."

"That's where I found you. You passed out. You gave me the scare of my life. Can you tell me what happened? How did you come by this cut on your arm? There are no teeth marks, so we can rule out an animal bite."

He was looking at me with such concern that my throat went dry. I looked away from him, and I tried to sound calm, "I was picking wildflowers. As I reached out to pick some beautiful ones off the path, a hidden branch caught me on the arm. I am sorry to have scared you," I said lamely. "The smell and sight of blood causes me to feel faint. Why did you take me to your shelter?"

"We were closer to this one," he answered, "and since I didn't know what was wrong, I didn't want to take any chances."

He had bandaged my arm, and there was no sight of blood.

"Thank you so much for taking care of me," I managed to say, trying to avoid his gaze. "I can get up now. I feel fine."

"OK," he said and removed his hand from my shoulder.

He straightened up and reached out a hand to help me up. I slowly got to my feet, a bit wobbly at first. He held onto me to make sure I was all right. We walked over to the table, and I sat down while he went to get me some water. A minute later he returned with the water. We sat in silence for a while. I was grateful that he had come along when he did. *Was he following me?* Anyway I was in no mood to fight at the moment. I sipped the water, thinking how different rainwater tasted, compared to regular water.

He spoke suddenly, breaking into my thoughts. "You shouldn't wander around alone; you are always so far away, with so much on your mind. What is it that brings such sadness to your eyes? How did you happen to be on this island? What are you running from?"

"Yes I do have quite a lot on my mind. I came to this island to escape and rest because everything in my world was crashing down on me. If you don't mind," I continued, "I really don't want to talk about it now. I just want to sit a while and enjoy this moment. My time here has been the happiest I have had in a long time. The thought of having to leave is always on my mind." The pain in my voice was getting too much for me. I couldn't trust myself to say more.

He said ever so softly. "You don't have to go." His dark eyes were searching my face.

"Yes, I have to go. There are things I need to attend to. I must go back and face the mess I left behind."

"Do you think you will come back?"

"I don't know, maybe. My life is quite complicated. I wish it were as simple as just dropping everything back there and staying here. I have grown to love this place and the wonderful people I have been with these past few days. I can't believe all that has happened in such short a time. It seems like I have been here for months. Yet, I have been here less than a week."

He sat quietly, looking at me without saying a word. I stopped talking suddenly. I realized I was going on and on. A little embarrassed, I made a move to get up. He reached out swiftly and took my hand.

"Don't stop," he said. "Your healing comes by letting it out."

He was so easy to talk to. As much as I wanted to talk, I knew that I should stop there.

Still holding onto my hand, he continued, "I don't mind listening."

"Thank you," I said, "but I must get back to the shelter."

"Not without me," he said, as he slowly got to his feet.

I was beginning to feel uncomfortable because he was still holding my hand and made no move to let go. I could feel the heat in the palm of my hand, and I know he felt it too. We stood looking at each other for a moment, as if everything had stopped and we were the only two people on the island. I shook my head to clear it, pulling my hand away. I stepped back from him toward the door.

We started back to the shelter in silence. The thought of what had just happened was still fresh in my mind. *What is he thinking? He is so quiet. Is he angry with me?* I couldn't tell. I had been trying to avoid his eyes since that awkward moment.

We were almost to the shelter when he asked, "Would you promise me something?"

Taken by surprise, I spun around to face him. "What?"

"That you won't go wandering around by yourself anymore."

"Why? What could happen to me on this small island?" I asked, smiling. He was not smiling. He looked so serious that he scared me.

"OK," I promised.

The look on his face didn't change. "When I found you today, I didn't know what to think. I felt so helpless. There you were, laid out on the ground with blood all over your arm. I thought I had lost you." His voice was so soft, barely a whisper. "That's why you shouldn't go out alone. I couldn't bear it if something should happen to you."

It was then that I realized he was getting too involved with me. I couldn't let that happen. Turning back to him, I said lightly, "You haven't told me anything about yourself. Have you always lived on the island? You want to know about me, and you haven't told me anything about yourself. Come on," I teased, "enough about me. Tell me about you."

Before we had a chance to continue, Gus joined us.

"Hi," he said smiling. Then he noticed the bandage on my arm. The smile was replaced by concern. "What happened to you?" he asked.

"Oh, I scraped my arm," I said. "It's nothing, and Doug bandaged it up."

Doug spoke up and said, "I found her passed out and bleeding by the roadside. I tried to tell her how dangerous it is for her to go running around here alone. Maybe you could talk some sense into her."

"Passed out! How did that happen?"

"I'll let Doug tell you about it. I am really tired."

I turned and walked away, feeling like a small, lost child and very tired. The events of the day had taken their toll on me. *Now, I will have to go over all this again with Mary, Vera, and Joe. Maybe I will just tell Mary. She can tell the others.* I walked inside to find that everyone was too busy to notice me. Breathing a sigh of relief, I walked to the far side of the shelter and sat down. Leaning my head back, I closed my eyes for a second to think about all that had happened since I left earlier.

I must have dozed off. When I opened my eyes again, it was almost dark. Doug was standing in front of me, blocking my view. "Do you feel better?" he asked. "I came by earlier to see if you wanted anything, but you were resting. I didn't have the heart to wake you."

"I do feel better," I stammered. "Please tell the others that I am fine. I really don't want them to worry about me—especially Mary—with all they have to deal with. If it's OK, I will just go curl up in my little corner and go to sleep."

He stood there looking at me. I couldn't see his face, but the tenderness in his voice made me feel uncomfortable again.

"Good night then. I will check on you in the morning."

With that he turned and walked away. I sat staring at his back. With his soft, gentle voice still ringing in my ears, I tried to get up and find my corner. I guess everyone knew what had happened to me by now. Just as I was about to fall asleep, Mary came over, looking worried.

"You all right, child? You gave us all quite a scare. The doctor is very worried about you," she said with a wink.

"I'm OK, Mary. I just need to sleep. I have not been sleeping well since the storm, and I have lots on my mind. I will feel better in the morning."

81

She brushed her hand gently across my forehead and smiled, "Good night, child." Then she walked away.

I was thankful for the quiet time to reflect on all that had happened. *How am I going to face Doug in the coming days? He is getting more and more interested in me. He seems to always be looking for me. I have to find some way to discourage him. It will not be easy; he is the kind of man who gets what he wants.*

I knew I could not entertain the feelings that were growing for him each day. As much as I wanted to forget my past, I knew that I must deal with it. Yet it would be so easy to continue to hide here and carry on with this simple way of life. I knew too well that my convictions wouldn't allow me to do that. Before drifting off to sleep, I whispered a prayer for strength.

For the first time since the storm, I had a good sleep. I opened my eyes to find that I was mostly alone. *Where is everyone? Is it that late?* I had slept for quite some time. Then I remembered how early people from the island got up. *Oh, well*, I thought, as I got to my feet.

The sun was up. It was going to be another beautiful day. I looked around for water, got cleaned up a bit, and then went to search for coffee. There it was, sitting on that round wood thing we called a table. *Thanks, Mary*, I whispered. She was so sweet, always looking out for me. She had made my coffee just the way I like it and was off somewhere. I sat enjoying the warm coffee and the quiet shelter.

13

DOUG'S
OWN STORM

*D*oug *finished his rounds at* his shelter, satisfied with the way his patients were recovering, and decided to go over to the other shelter. He was struggling with his feelings for Deborah. He couldn't seem to get her out of his mind.

It had been so long since he felt this way about a woman. Yet, he thought, *I don't know anything about her. What is her story? What is she running from? This is crazy! This is not me. I don't fall this easily.* His thoughts went back to when he found her after she had passed out by the path. She looked so helpless. He could not forget the pain in his heart. It felt as if something had pulled his heart right out of his chest. *I promised myself I would never go through this again. Here I am, falling in love with someone I don't even know.*

He entered the shelter to find Deborah sitting at the far corner, her back to him. He stood in the doorway, looking at her, and thought, *She is such a beautiful woman, with long black hair flowing down the middle of her back. Her dark, almost smoky eyes seem to see right through me. She is so fragile in many ways, yet so strong when she needs to be.*

It took every bit of his willpower not to go over to her and stroke her hair and tell her everything would be all right. He also knew this wouldn't go over well with her. He remembered the sadness in her voice when he had asked about her past. He knew she needed time to think and sort out whatever it was that hurt so much. Collecting his thoughts, he walked over to his patients. Deeply involved with his work, he didn't notice that she had walked out of the shelter.

Debby

Finishing my coffee, I put my cup down and started for the door. I noticed that Doug had come in and was taking care of the injured. I decided to slip out before he had a chance to see me. I couldn't face him now—not yet. I needed some time to think.

Maybe I should just find a way to get out of here before things get out of hand. He is such a nice, caring guy. I can't bear the thought of hurting him. I do have feelings for him, but they must never come to the surface. I still don't know anything about him, and he seems very reluctant to talk about himself. Yet, when I am in his presence, his voice, his good looks, and his soft brown eyes seem to make me forget my problems.

I sat daydreaming about how easy it would be live here—maybe get myself a little house and start all over. It would be so wonderful to be able to spend time in the sun, take long walks, pick wildflowers, and go swimming in the ocean all year round. It had never taken much to make me happy. I had always been a happy person till everyone started taking me for granted. I felt I had become a part of the furniture. So much was expected from me, yet no one cared how I felt. Plans were made for me, and I had no say about them. The idea of my running around like a robot made me cringe.

Does anyone miss me? Are they getting along without me? They will have to, because right now, I don't think I will ever go back. No one should have to live like that. I did it for too many years. It's the most horrible feeling to be with people who claim to love you, yet hardly notice that you're around or appreciate the things you do. It's almost like you're a shadow. What a sad way to live! I know if I hadn't left I would have died.

Thinking about it now brought the pain back all over again. I pushed it out of my mind, trying to forget it for the time being. But I could sense that the time was coming when I would have to deal with it.

Doug was right. Talking about my struggles will bring healing. I should get back so he can have a look at my arm. I left so quickly he didn't have a chance. He must be looking for me by now. I promised him I wouldn't go wandering around by myself. I jumped to my feet, realizing that I had been gone longer than I expected.

Doug hastily put his things away, hoping she hadn't gone too far. He was hurrying out the door when he bumped into Gus.

"What's your hurry?" Gus called after him.

"I need to find Deborah, to check on her arm. Have you seen her?"

"No," Gus said, "When I left this morning, she was still asleep. Would you like me to go find her?"

"No!" Doug said a bit too quickly. "I will find her." Seeing the surprised look on Gus's face, he went on to say, "It's just that I am worried about her, with what happened yesterday and all." With that he took off and left Gus standing there, wondering what in the world was going on.

Doug's mind was in turmoil as he hurried on. *Where can she be? One minute she was there, and the next she was gone.* He couldn't believe how worried he was that something might happen to her. He blamed himself for not letting her know he was there. *If only I had gone over and talked to her, looked at her arm, she might not be out there now. She is so high-spirited and has a mind of her own. She's not like any woman I have ever known.* He was so caught up in his thoughts he didn't see her sitting on a log up ahead.

Debby

The look on Doug's face told me I was in for another lecture. As he got closer, I couldn't tell if the look was relief or frustration.

"Hi," I said smiling.

He looked at me with his dark, piercing eyes and said, "I was looking for you to check your arm."

"It's OK. You don't need to."

"I need to look at it to make sure it's healing right. You don't want a nasty, big scar on your arm now, do you?"

"I guess not," I said.

"Where do you want to do this?"

He pointed to the tree trunk I had been sitting on earlier. We walked the few steps back and sat down. He reached over and started taking the bandage off. He was so gentle that I didn't feel a thing. I had my eyes closed. If there was any blood, I didn't want to faint again.

"There," he said after a few minutes. "Everything looks good. You are healing well. You won't need a bandage, but try to keep it clean."

"Will do!" I said lightly. As I started to get to my feet, he caught my hand suddenly.

"We have to talk," he said.

I stood looking at him, speechless. The look in his eyes scared me. *Oh no!* I thought. *Not now. I can't do this. He is too serious. This is not good.* My head was spinning; I felt dizzy.

"About what?" I managed to say.

"About us!" He went on to say, "You must know how I feel about you. I can't get you out of my mind. You consume my days!"

"Stop!" I shouted. "You don't know anything about me. This is happening too fast. Please, there is so much that I need to sort

86

out. I am still trying to find out who I am."

To my surprise, he gently pulled me close to him and held me. At that moment I felt so safe; it would have been easy to forget all my problems.

He said, in a voice that was barely a whisper, "Take all the time you need. I can wait."

It took all the strength I could find to pull away from him. Feeling a bit embarrassed, I mumbled something about having to get back to the shelter.

"I'll walk back with you," he said lightly.

We walked in silence for a while, not trusting ourselves to say any more. It felt so good just to walk with him, not having to feel self-conscious in his presence.

I said shyly, "Do you mind if we were just friends for now?"

"That would be fine," he answered, "as long as you remember how I feel about you. I will give you as much time as you need, but I hope you will learn to trust me. Tell me what it is that hurt you so. It tears me apart to see you in so much pain. Won't you please tell me about it? Where do you come from? And what are you running from? You know, you don't have to carry it alone. Whatever it is, I will be with you. Nothing you have done could change the way I feel about you."

He continued on as though driven to pour out his heart. "I don't fall in love easily. It only happened once before, and I swore it wouldn't happen again. Then you came along out of nowhere and stole my heart. From the moment I set eyes on you, I knew I was in trouble."

Feeling the need to divert his mind from me, I asked shyly, "What happened to your first love?"

He looked away, staring in the distance. After what seemed like a long pause, he turned around to face me. By the look on his face, I could tell that he was struggling with his emotions. I was sorry I had asked.

I spoke up quickly. "It's OK if you don't want to talk about it."

When he spoke again, his voice was a mask of pain. "As a

young boy growing up on the island of St. Ann's, I had big dreams. I always wanted to be a doctor. Being the only son of a merchant gave me lots of opportunity to meet people from the other islands. I love my island and its people. I felt that if I could be a doctor, I could come back and help my people.

"After school on St. Ann's, I went to the States— New York— to study. It was there that I met my wife. She was so beautiful, with a rich island background. Though she wasn't born on the island, her parents were. We made great plans to come back and work together. We lived in the States for a while after I finished my internship. Then we decided to return.

"Things went well for a while. We were very much in love. Though she was a surgical nurse, she decided to stay at home and become a mom. I guess it was my fault. I was away from home a lot, traveling to the other islands and sometimes staying at them a week or more at a time. When I got home, she would want to tell me all that had happened while I was gone. I would rush around and put her off. I always had something to do, and I never realized how lonely she was. By this time we had two children. Our son, Raymond, was three and our daughter, Fay, one.

"One day, she was gone. I never saw it coming. At first I was angry with her for giving up all that we had worked to build. I thought if that was what she wanted, then that was fine. I buried myself in my work. My mother took care of our children. Every day I came home, hoping she would be there, but she never came back. We never heard a word from her. Our children grew up and are now studying in the States." He paused for a bit, the pain still in his eyes.

"Did you try to find her?" I asked.

"At first I didn't. Then, when it was painfully evident that she wasn't coming back, I tried to find her. I went back to the States, but no one had seen or heard from her. It's as if she had disappeared. I was beside myself with worry. What if something had happened to her? What if she was hurt and not able to get in touch with me? Those thoughts almost drove me mad."

I couldn't help it. I had to ask, "And to this day you still don't know what has happened to her?"

"No," he said slowly.

"But what if she lost her memory and doesn't know who she is?"

"That thought stayed with me a long, long time, and over the years I have hoped to one day run into her on the street. But this was twenty years ago. That is why, when I first saw you, I acted so strange. You look a bit like her. You were standing in the shadow, with just a flicker of light to illumine you. I stood looking at you, not trusting myself to move. Then you turned, and I knew it wasn't her. Don't you see? You brought to the surface feelings I had buried for so long, never trusting myself to love again."

"So you don't love me. You're still in love with her."

"Don't be silly. I am in love with you! I would have never told you all this if I didn't love you. I wanted you to know all about me so there won't be any secrets between us."

I thought, *if only he knew how similar our stories are.* Then my heart went out to him. I couldn't help feeling the pain of his wife. *I wonder what happened to her.* This brought me back to my family. *Is anyone looking for me? Do they notice that I am gone?*

I didn't have much time to brew over it because Mary joined us, looking very worried. "Where did you disappear to this time?" she asked, shaking her finger at me. "You know we all worry about you. You left this morning, and now you coming back."

She was scolding me like I was a child. I felt a little embarrassed, but I let her go on. I knew she was worried about me. I managed to say weakly, "I'm sorry, Mary. I didn't mean to make you worry."

"That's all right, child. Now, come eat!"

Doug stood looking on with a grin, knowing it was entirely his fault. We followed Mary into the shelter, and everyone looked up as we walked in. Gus looked at us with a knowing smile. I found a seat near Joe. I hadn't seen him in a while, and I wanted to find out how he was doing. He smiled and looked up as I approached.

"I see Mary let you have it," he said. "She means well. She was fussing about you all morning."

"I know. It's my fault. I should have come back sooner. But that's enough about me. Tell me about yourself. What have you been up to?"

"Well, the boys and I are trying to put some of the broken houses back together," he said. "That way we don't all have to be crammed into this shelter. We are also putting a proper shower together so you ladies can have some privacy."

"Oh, that will be so nice," I replied. "Thank you so much, Joe."

He looked at me, his bright eyes beaming. I couldn't help it. I reached over and kissed him lightly on his face. He was all embarrassed and looked around nervously to see if anyone was looking. Satisfied that no one had seen it, he continued to eat.

Lunch was great. I stood up and walked over to where Mary stood talking to Vera. Gus and Doug were busy talking. Mary looked up and smiled.

"You a-right, child?" she asked in her singsong tone.

"Yep," I replied. "I will be outside taking in the breeze in case you need me."

With that, I walked out. A little ways from the shelter, I found a shady spot and sat down. I felt so full from lunch that I wanted to take a nap. Leaning my head back, I closed my eyes.

Thoughts of Doug came flowing back to my mind. The pain in his eyes as he spoke about his wife left no doubt in my mind that he was still in love with her. How horrible it must have been for him to come back and find her gone. The children grew up without knowing what had happened to their mother. He never said what he told them about her disappearance. I didn't have the heart to ask.

This brought me back to my own problems. *What is going on at home? Is my husband going through the same grief and pain?* Before I had a chance to dwell on it further, Mary broke into my thoughts.

14

Mary's Words
of Wisdom

Debby

"You sleeping, child?"

"No, just daydreaming. Sit with me a while," I invited.

"Well a-right," she said, sitting down.

She was looking at me as if she had something on her mind. "What is it, Mary? What's troubling you?"

A bit shy, she said, "It's you, child. You are so troubled with so much on your mind. What is it that brings such sadness to your eyes? When you don't know, I am watching, I see the tears in your eyes. It's almost like something is hurting real bad."

Her soft, motherly voice opened the dam again. The tears started to flow. She reached over and held me, "There now, let it all out."

I don't know how long I cried. It seemed forever. Still holding me, she asked softly, "Do you want to talk about it?" I nodded, pulling back and wiping my eyes.

"Oh, Mary," I said, a bit shaken. "I don't know where to start."

"Go on, child," she urged. "Take your time."

"You are right. I am running away from my life. I am the wife of a pastor. We run a very large church in Boston. My husband is a very busy man, and I seem to be in his shadow most of the time. It was not always this way.

"We were very much in love at one time. At first, I was very happy to be part of his life and work. Then we got very involved in church ministry. As the years went on, we found ourselves working more and more apart. I tried to talk with him about what was going on with me, but he never had the time to listen.

"I got to the place where I felt that I had become his live-in maid. I prayed and asked the Lord to do something about it. This is what we are taught to do. Things grew worse. We got to the place where we never saw each other for days. I would hear all about the nice things he was saying about me, but never to me. I felt that I had become part of his achievements. I buried myself in ministry, hoping the pain and loneliness would go away. I was not the kind of woman to look at another man. Yet, I had plenty of opportunity.

"There was no one to talk to about what I was going through. The people around us were always giving me compliments about what a great man my husband was. They had no idea how sad and lonely I was. I felt myself dying a little each day. It was then that I decided to go away— so far away that no one would find me. I felt that my husband had left me for the church, and the Lord allowed it to happen. As far as I was concerned, I didn't have a husband. That's my story."

"O, you poor child," she said after a while. "Now I see. But don't for a moment think that the good Lord left you. Didn't He keep you safe in this storm? He has been watching over you all this time. He will make it right, you'll see. You will have to contact your husband and tell him where you are. He must be worried sick about you, with the storm and all."

"I did leave him a note. He will find me if he wants to. Somehow I doubt if he will bother. He is too busy with his TV and radio programs to care about me."

She looked at me sadly and said, "I can't understand how a man could be so wrapped up in himself and not take care of what he promised to cherish." We sat in silence for a while. Then I spoke, breaking the silence. "Did you know about Doug's wife?"

"Yes, child. All the island people know."

"What do you suppose happened to her?"

"Some said that she took off with another man. Others say she just got tired and left. But no one has seen her since she left."

"Did you know her?" I asked curiously.

"No, I never met her," she answered.

"Poor man," I said. "He still carries the pain."

"That is true," she continued. "That is why I am worried about you. You do know that he is in love with you. You are all he talks about. He has asked everyone about you."

"Oh, Lord, what am I to do? I tried to tell him that it would be of no use. I also tried to tell him that I have another life. He wouldn't listen. What can I do? I really don't want to hurt him. I do have feelings for him, but they must never come to the surface. I am still a married woman, in spite of what I am going through. I have to be careful not to lead him on."

"That's a very wise choice, child," she said with a smile. "You must tell him as soon as possible, so he won't get his hopes up. You know the good Lord will make a way."

"You know, Mary, I don't think he is in love with me. He is in love with the memory of his missing wife. He said I reminded him of her. I think he is still in love with her. Maybe one day she will show up, and he will be happy again. He is a great guy. He deserves some happiness. The guilt he's lived with all these years must be a nightmare. The last thing I want to do now is to add to his pain."

The thought came back to me about how similar Doug's situation and mine were. *Is the Lord allowing this to happen so we can find the true meaning of His plans for us? Everything I have been taught goes against this way of thinking. The Bible school teaches that we are to follow our husband and smile at him no matter what. Well, I tried that, and it was killing me.*

I have always believed that God means it when He says in the

93

Word that the man should love his wife the way Christ loves his church. I can't understand how it is possible for men of God to preach to others about loving their wives and then treat their wives as second-class Christians. For years I have seen this in the church. As a girl, I always said this would never happen to me. Boy, was I wrong!

When I met and fell in love with Andy, he was so different. He had a great sense of humor. I remember walking into his lecture after it had already started. He turned around as I walked in, and everything stopped. He stood looking at me with his mouth open, completely at a loss for words. He was so funny that everyone turned around to see who or what he was looking at. I was so embarrassed. It makes me smile now to think about it.

We didn't date long. He was older than I was, and he made a point to let me know he wanted to marry me. He didn't have time for a long courtship. He was a serious man of God. He knew what he wanted, and he didn't have time to play around. I loved that in him. We had a quiet wedding a month after we met. Everyone said we should have waited. Andy wouldn't hear of it. He had made up his mind that I was the one he wanted. I was so smitten by him that I would have followed him to the moon.

With his high spirits, his great sense of humor, and the way he was so wrapped up with the Lord, it was as if God was his best friend. This was something I had not seen in all my years in the church. He talked to the Lord and expected an answer. All this was new to me. The way he dealt with religious people was something else. His favorite saying was, "The Lord is not in religion! He is into relationships. The churches have it wrong." We had a great time serving the Lord; we were happy. I had never known anyone like him. Then it happened. We got big, and I lost him to the church.

I didn't realize I was thinking out loud until Mary said, "He sounds like quite a guy."

I was so far away into my past that I had forgotten about Mary. As I struggled to come back to the present, she continued, "Just like Doug, you are still in love with your Andy. I truly believe that the good Lord allowed this storm to come so we all could deal with the storms in our lives. I think you will find that your Andy is very worried about you and is doing everything he can to get to you. The good Lord will bring him here. You'll see," she said with a smile.

She was right. *Andy is the kind of man who would do just that. He knows the islands, and being a mission pilot, it won't take him long to find me— that's if he even cares anymore.* I was starting to get down again. *Maybe, he is too wrapped up in whatever he is doing to think about me. I will have to try to forget for now and see what the next few days bring for me.*

Mary was looking at me with a twinkle in her soft dark eyes. "Your Andy will come and take you home. Don't worry."

She was so confident in what she believed that it made me dare to hope.

"We should be getting back," she said suddenly. "The others will be looking for us."

"Before we go," I asked, "Will you pray with me?"

"I have been praying for you all along, child. I noticed how sad you were and the great burden you were carrying. I knew you would talk about it when the time was right. I always prayed that the good Lord would give you the strength to deal with what was troubling you, that He would bring peace and contentment to your heart."

"Oh, thank you so very much, Mary," I stammered, "I believe it was your prayers that kept me together."

"Then let's pray, child!" She thanked the good Lord for His love, protection, mercy, and grace, but most of all for Jesus. She went on to ask the Lord to bring Andy safely through in his search for me.

I jumped in when she was finished and said, "Lord, please forgive me for being so stubborn. Help me to understand Your plans for my life. And Lord, please let Doug find out something about his wife."

"Amen!" Mary said joyfully.

We started back to the shelter. I found myself smiling, thinking about Andy.

Mary turned to me abruptly. "What you think about Joe and me getting together?" She continued before I had a chance to respond. "We are both old, and our children have their own lives. I am very fond of him, and I know he likes me."

"I think you make a great couple. Joe is such a nice, gentle person, and you are the kindest person I have ever met. I think that's great—you two together."

Mary beamed like a schoolgirl. "Thank you so much," she said. "It makes me so happy that you approve."

We entered the shelter to find the men sitting around talking. Vera was busy cooking in the far corner, and Mary hurried over to give her a hand. It was good to see Vera taking care of things without being asked.

The shelter almost looked like a house now, with the men working so hard to make it comfortable. Joe had made a small building for us to take showers. On the top he had placed a large drum to catch rainwater. He, along with the others, had made some little beds for us so we wouldn't have to lie on the cold floor. They had found some of the broken furniture and had put most of it back together so it could be used. We now had a few more chairs, a couple of tables, more spoons and knives. Almost all the sheets and blankets, though muddy and wet when we found them, were now washed and clean. There was a lightness about the place now, a feeling of home.

I looked over to where the men were. To my surprise, Doug sat staring at me, not paying any attention to the others. The look in his eyes was too much for me to handle. I turned around abruptly and walked out the door.

I need to settle this with him soon. I can't go through this much longer. Now, with my thoughts all mixed up about Andy, I can't even think straight. How, I thought, *am I going to tell Doug about Andy? With all he's been through, this will hurt him and maybe even turn him away from women for good. Yet, I am not the one he's in love with. That should make it easier to tell him.*

Oh Lord, how did I get myself into this? I prayed.

15

FLIGHT
TO ST. ANN'S

Andy

I awoke—*if I really ever slept*—just as the sun was coming up.
After finding a small coffee shop at the airport, I bought a
dozen coffees and a box of donuts and then went back and woke
up the crew. The tower was just opening after we finished our
meager breakfast, so we gave them a few minutes to get organized
and called for clearances. By the time the clearances crackled
back on the radios, all our planes were warmed up and ready.

We took off one after another, with the Commander and the
Caravan going on ahead. When we landed at St. Ann's about
an hour and a half later, we found the runway clear, although
debris lined both sides of it. We were shown to a parking area
and the local ground crew recognized the emblem on our planes
and welcomed us. After explaining that more planes were coming behind us, we asked for a place where we could set up a
temporary base.

An older man disappeared and then returned to direct us to
an empty hangar that wasn't too badly damaged. He apologized
for its condition, but we assured him that it was fine. The power

97

hadn't returned yet, but it had several rooms in the back and was perfect for a small barracks and offices. It would work OK. We began cleaning it up immediately. Within minutes, we heard the roar of the DC-3s landing, followed by the C-206.

By midafternoon we were ready to start operations. Volunteers had come from a local church. The first plane out was the single engine Cessna 206, loaded to the max. It was going to a nearby island with an airport. An hour later I went to another in almost the opposite direction. By evening we were back and preparing for the next day.

Later that night, several customs officials visited us and offered to help cut the considerable red tape that always slows down relief operations like ours. I was talking to one of them, showed him Debby's picture, and asked if he had seen her. He called over his friend.

They both talked together for a minute then said, "Yes, mon. She is a beautiful woman, mon, but she so sad, mon."

"You saw her? When? Where is she?" I blurted. "She was sad? How?"

"Her eyes, mon. We saw her three days before the storm. Slow down, mon. She left the next day on a boat. That is why I talked to my friend. He is customs for boats, mon."

"Where did she go?"

"She took a small coastal island boat to the south, mon," answered the friend. "When I asked for her destination, she only said, 'Someplace quiet.' There are many quiet islands in that direction. The storm smash them up, mon."

I reached for a steel barrel to lean on. I had just heard the news I dreaded most.

"Why you so interested in this island woman, mon?" the first customs man asked.

"She is my wife," I squeezed out.

"We are sorry, mon. If we can help, we will see what we can find."

I thanked them and sat down. I couldn't think. I could hardly breathe. Jake had overheard the discussion and came up.

"Don't lose it now, Andy. It's not over till it's over, and we just got here. We'll find her, and she'll be OK. Remember, she belongs to God as well as you. He has known her much longer than you have. You've got to trust now, and we will get to work first light."

I grabbed him and just held onto him for a minute. I could see the other guys agreeing and offering all their help.

Thank you, Lord, for them. I do believe we will find her, I prayed.

16

BONE-BREAKING DENGUE FEVER

Debby

Food was the furthest thing from my mind at the moment. I walked back in to find that everyone was already eating. Mary handed me a plate, and everything looked so good. I had always enjoyed fish fried in coconut oil, with green bananas and all the other roots they eat here but I wasn't hungry.

I sat staring at the food on my plate, feeling a bit sick. *Oh no, I am going to be sick.* I put my plate down and ran outside, barely making it to the side of the shelter before I brought everything up. I was leaning up against the shelter, sweat pouring from my face. I felt dizzy, as chills shot through my body. I didn't know Mary had followed me until she wrapped her arms around me to stop me from shaking. She wiped my face with the hem of her dress, and we headed back inside. I was leaning heavily on her, and she partly carried me.

Everyone looked up with great concern as we entered. Doug jumped to his feet and half ran across the room. He reached out to help Mary, and as she let go of me, I passed out. I woke to find Doug sitting on a chair near my little bed. His eyes were closed, I wondered if he was sleeping. He looked so tired. *How long has he been sitting there? And how long was I out? The last thing I remember, he was walking toward Mary and me. Then everything went black. Not again,* I thought. *This is getting to be a problem.*

I didn't have much time to think about it. Just then he opened his eyes and looked at me. He caught me staring at him. Embarrassed, I tried to look away.

"How do you feel?" he asked.

"Like a train ran me over," I said. "How long have I been out?"

"A couple of days. You had a touch of fever—what is known as dengue."

"What in the world is that? I've never heard of it."

"It comes from mosquito bites," he said lightly. "You gave us quite a scare. We were all worried about you. You will have to stay in bed and rest a day or two. There is no real cure for it except rest."

Looking at him, I couldn't help noticing how tired he looked. His eyes were bloodshot, and he didn't look his normal self. As he sat back down, I asked, "When was the last time you slept? Have you been here with me all this time?"

A lazy grin crossed his face. "Don't worry about me. You rest now and get better."

"Please go lie down and get some rest. I will be fine. Besides, I have Mary to take care of me." Mary walked in just as I was speaking.

"Well," she said, "it's good to see you up. You gave us a real scare."

Mary was so happy to see me awake. Then she looked at Doug, who was half-asleep in the chair.

"Off you go, Doc. You need some sleep."

He looked over at me, reluctant to leave.

"I will be fine," I said. "Go on."

He slowly got up and walked out. Pulling the chair closer to the bed, Mary sat down.

"Doug was beside himself with worry," she said. "He never

left your side. He stayed with you the whole time you were out. I had to almost drag him out of here to eat. When you passed out and he didn't know what was wrong, he was going out of his mind. He carried you in here so gently and laid you down as if you were the most precious thing. He kept putting cold compresses on your face."

"And there is something else. You talked a lot. You kept calling him Andy."

"Oh, no! That's why he was looking at me so strangely this morning."

Oh great! I thought. *Now I have to tell him about Andy. That won't be easy. How did I ever allow things to get so out of hand? Maybe if I just lie here and close my eyes, all this will go away. That would be nice, but somehow I don't think it will be that easy. Doug will never let me forget it. Besides, I can't get away from him since I am laid up like this. And watchdog Mary would have my hide if I tried to get past her. What am I going to do?* With that I dozed off.

17

JAKE'S STORY

Andy

The next several days were very hard. We loaded the planes at night if there was enough light or at the first light of day at 5 a.m. We flew to so many devastated islands. The hard part was not only ten to twelve hours in a cockpit, sometimes with only six hours of sleep. It also included a diet of stale sandwiches and flat, warm sodas and the task of unloading cargoes of food, medicine, drinking water, and other relief supplies, as much as the planes could handle.

We could never carry enough. Many times we were overloaded, gambling with our capability to get the heavy planes into the air. We had not as yet reached all the smaller islands, and all we could do was to give what we could to people on the islands we did visit and promise to come back with more. So far, we had not been able to make repeat flights. We were totally overwhelmed. The two DC-3s ran a continuous flight back and forth, bringing in more supplies. Our ground crews labored day and night with very little sleep, working to keep the aircraft ready, loaded, and serviced.

Everywhere I landed, I showed Debby's picture and asked if

anyone had seen her. No one had, and I was getting frantic. *Where is she? Is she OK, still alive?*

One evening on the way back in, I thought, *Hey! What's wrong with me? I'll ask the boat customs officer to take me to the boat captain, and he'll tell me which island he left her at. Yeah!* I was kicking myself the rest of the way down.

As I cleared customs at the airport, I asked the aviation customs officer how I could get in touch with his friend who worked customs for the boats. He got on the phone that had just been restored the day before and called his friend.

"Mon, he'll be over in a little while. He is just finishing his shift for the day."

"Great! I'll sit here and wait."

"Mon, do you want a cup of coffee? I just made a fresh pot."

"Why yes, I think I need some."

"Mon, you look like you need a lot more than just coffee. I understand you guys are flying almost continuous. You look like you don't sleep, mon. You lost weight since last week, and don't get vexed, mon, but you need to bathe."

Laughing, I replied, "Guilty on all accounts."

He laughed and handed me a steaming cup of coffee. I took a swallow, and my eyes popped open in a knee-jerk reaction. It had the consistency of watery mud.

"We should bottle this stuff. It would *have* to cure something."

"Yes, mon," he laughed. "Sleep."

"Mon, have you heard anything about your wife?" He asked in a serious voice.

"No, not yet, I've landed on maybe a dozen islands, but no one has seen her. That's why I want to talk to your friend again. I thought if I could find the boat captain she sailed with, maybe he could tell me where he landed her."

"Hmm... good idea, mon. Why didn't I think of that?"

"That's what I said as I was flying back."

"Hey mon, here he comes."

After the usual handshaking and pleasantries, I was anxious

to ask him my question. "I was thinking, could you introduce me to the captain of the boat Debby went on? Maybe he would remember the island where he left her."

The boat customs officer became quiet. Finally, after a long silence he said, "Mon, the boat didn't come back. We have not heard from it. I hoped I would get better news before I had to tell you. I'm real sorry, mon."

To say that I crashed and burned is an understatement. All I could do was stand there as the reality sank in. I had spied a glimmer of hope and put all my trust in it. Once again I had put my trust in the wrong place. I mumbled my thanks and said I had to get back to the hangar. They also mumbled something I didn't catch, and I left. I walked back to the hangar, and Jake saw me in the distance. He hurried toward me.

"You OK?"

"Yeah, I guess so."

I told him what happened. We went in to catch a bite to eat, but I didn't eat much. After we sat in silence a while, I got up and went to my bunk in the barracks. Jake followed me. I turned to him and just blankly stared. "I can't continue like this. I'm burned-out! I'm a total wreck," I blurted out.

Jake sat down on a bunk and listened patiently as I went through a whole list of things. I had a total pity party. "I this... I that... why me? What did I do to God to bring all this on me? Why Debby? All we ever did was try to serve Him." It went on and on. Finally I ran out of energy and words. I just stood there. I couldn't even cry. There wasn't anything left. Jake just sat there.

After what seemed like hours, he spoke quietly. "You need some rest. I'm going to ground you for a few days."

"You can't do that. I need to keep looking. I'm one of the best pilots you have. I know these islands like the palm of my hand."

"Yes, I can. And if you don't pull yourself together, you won't be flying for us at all. First, I can't take a chance that you might wallow in your pity party and put a hole in the water. I need that plane, and I really need you. But unless you get it together, you are useless.

"Hundreds of families out there have lost loved ones and heads of households. Who is going to take care of them? There isn't a welfare system here, and without food or medicine they are left to die. For many, we are their only living hope. Their governments were almost destroyed, and even those that survived cannot cope with a disaster of this magnitude.

"You haven't got word about Debby? Well, keep trusting in the very God you were questioning. At least you have the hope she has survived somewhere. How many here have no hope left? I sit here listening to you. Yes, you are tired and worried, but man, you can still fight the fight. Don't lose because you just quit. I've got things to do. I'll be back. Get a shower."

With that he left.

I sat down, wallowing in my pity party. I knew he was right. As long as you can get up and keep going, you're not finished. I might not have good news, but I didn't have any bad news either. *Why couldn't he have been gentler? Is this what I needed? I guess I needed a dose of reality.* I was still numb. My mind was in confusion.

I went in and took a shower in cold water (we only had cold water). It actually helped clear my mind some. I knew I couldn't stop looking for Debby, but I had to get my act together. Jake was right. I was so involved with my own problems that I was closing out all that I saw around me. I sat for a while, trying not to think. I was so tired...so tired. It was like everything inside was drying up. I had run into a wall. I couldn't go any further.

I cried out desperately in a loud voice, "Lord! I can't do this by myself. I need Your help." The sound of my voice shocked me. I felt the Lord's peace come over me again. In my self-pity I had lost trust, then hope, and finally peace. "Lord, thank You again, I will continue to try. I can do it with Your help."

A few minutes later Jake returned. I looked at him and said, "Before you say anything, thank you. I guess I needed that."

"Yeah, you did. I needed it once too a long time ago. I also had a friend who cared enough to tell me the truth. It was John. Many years ago in my early twenties, I was a hotshot pilot. I had come to the mission just to build flight time so I could eventually fly for the airlines. I had been married only six months."

"In all these years I've known you, I never knew you were married."

"Yeah, I know. April used to fly with me the same way Debby did with you. One day a friend of hers from school called. Her friend was going on a Caribbean cruise she had won. They arranged to meet in one of the big hotels on a French resort island. I was flying further down island, so it worked out perfectly. I would drop April off and pick her up the next evening on my way back. Everything was just great."

I sat mesmerized. This was a Jake I didn't know.

"The next day, about four o'clock in the afternoon, the girls were taking a last walk down the beach. They went further then the rest of the tourists. A Rasta man came out from some sea grape bushes and attacked them both with a cutlass. It was only because they were on his part of the beach. He didn't own it or anything. It was just his because he was born there on the island.

"My wife was DOA at the hospital. I arrived forty-five minutes later and was taken to the hospital. I found out that April was carrying our first child. The police caught the Rasta man, and he was tried and found guilty. I didn't go to the trial."

Jake spoke in a matter-of-fact tone. All emotion had long since been dealt with. I could not look at him. I was in shock.

Jake drank a glass of water and then started again.

"I was in total shock. The doctors gave me a shot to put me out. I woke the next day, and John was sitting by my bed. I looked at him and just broke down and wept. John didn't say anything. He just put his arms around me and held me like a father holds his son. I don't know how long I wept, but when I finally slowed down, I noticed that John had been weeping too.

"He and Barbara helped me through it over a period of time. I was full of bitterness and hate. They taught me how to forgive.

One day, John gave me a speech similar to the one I gave you tonight. I decided to dedicate my life through Jesus Christ to these island people who have struggled so many hundreds of years to have better lives.

"I am here with you, Andy, but you have to let me in to help. I want to find Debby too. I don't want to lose another... friend. Now you know."

I was at a loss for words. "Jake, forgive me. Help me be strong. I need to find Debby."

"No need to forgive because there is nothing to forgive. I already said I would, and I am helping. Are you ready to go back to work, or do you need a few days off?"

"I... I think so."

"Just promise me that you will ground yourself if you get out of control— or I will."

"I'll try," I said stronger.

"OK, let's get to work. I have the charts laid out, and the islands we have already been to are marked. Let's take a look. I'm sending the Cessna 206 and the Commander to islands that have runways, and you to ones that don't. The other guys have been showing her picture on every island they have visited. There aren't many left."

"I didn't know they were doing that. Where did they get the pictures?"

"John sent them down. I told you we were all helping. You aren't a Lone Ranger, you know. It's getting late, so hit the sack. We'll get a fresh start at first light."

I walked back to the barracks, thinking that I had once again been a fool. *Here all the guys are looking for Debby too. Wow! I'm supposed to be the great leader. It shows that we all need each other much more than we think.* I was still shaken by Jake's story. I had known him many years and had no idea of the loss and pain he had suffered. I felt my hope being renewed again. I cleaned up and went to bed. I fell asleep almost immediately.

18

THE MOMENT
OF TRUTH

*D*oug *barely made it back* to his shelter where he found his sleeping spot and went right to sleep. Thoughts of Deborah going on and on about a guy named Andy were in his dreams. He woke with a start and for a moment did not remember where he was. He had been running ragged for some time now, and with the epidemic of dengue fever in both shelters, he was having a hard time getting any sleep. He lay there for a while, thinking how good it was to finally get some rest.

Again his thoughts went back to Deborah. He felt a knot in his stomach as he remembered the way she kept calling for Andy. *Who is this Andy anyway?* He had to know, and right away! Yet, he wasn't sure he was ready to handle the knowledge of who this guy is. Questions kept swirling through his mind. *Is this the reason for her reluctance to talk about herself? Is this her reason for being on this island? Why is she running away from him? And, if she is, why would she call for him? Is she afraid of this guy? Or is she in love with him?*

He realized he was driving himself crazy by thinking this way, but he couldn't stop. He slowly got out of bed, thinking he should go check up on Deborah. Yet, this was something he wasn't looking forward to. Maybe she was doing better today, and he wouldn't have to face her. He got himself a cup of coffee and sat down, hoping to wake up a bit before checking on his patients.

Sipping his coffee slowly, his thoughts went back to the first time he had seen her. *Oh no,* he told himself, *not again!* Shaking his head to clear his mind, he got up suddenly and walked over to his first patient. Everyone was doing well. Some of the injured were walking around, and even those who had suffered the most severe injuries were off the critical list. It would soon be time for him to go back to the main island.

It sure would be nice if Deborah could go back with him. The first time he met her he knew she would become a part of his life. He didn't want to fall in love with her. He just wanted to get to know her. Yet, here he was, head over heels in love with her. *What am I going to do?* he asked himself. *No matter how hard I try, I can't get her out of my mind.*

As he struggled to keep his mind on his work, the name *Andy* kept coming back to him. He decided to get this thing about Andy straightened out today. He made up his mind to go have a talk with Deborah. After he had checked on all his patients, he grabbed his bag and walked out the door.

Debby

"Yuck," I said, as I saw Mary carrying a hot bowl of soup and some bush tea to me. "Not that bush tea again."

"Yes, child, you must drink this if you want to get better. This tea is the only thing that will work on this dengue fever. Here in the island we call it 'the bone-breaking fever.' Now hush! Drink your tea before it gets cold. It tastes real bad when you drink it cold."

"I didn't think it could get any worse," I mumbled. I held my breath and swallowed as fast as I could, thinking all the time, *this tastes bad enough to kill me.* Mary stood smiling as I handed her the empty cup.

"That's a good girl," she said. "I'll have you up and about in no time. Now eat your soup."

With that, she walked out of the room. *Bone-breaking indeed! Everywhere hurts,* I thought. *All I can do is try and stay as still as possible. That isn't easy.* I forced myself to eat the soup, trying not to gag. *Mary has gone to so much trouble to make this. The best I can do is to eat it.*

Putting the bowl down, I laid back on the lump that was a pillow, hoping to get back to sleep. *All one can do with this fever is sleep,* I thought. *Thank God for Mary! She's been going around looking after everyone. I hope she is immune to this fever. She's lived on this island a long time, and I'm sure she's had it once or twice. But if she must get it again, please let me get well first so I can take of her,* I prayed as I drifted off to sleep.

When I opened my eyes, the shelter was mostly dark. *This means the sun is going down. I missed the outdoors, the thing I like most about this island. The beautiful sunset can make you forget your troubles.* I was so deep in thought that I didn't see Doug standing in the shadow. "You startled me," I said, trying to sound calm. "How long have you been standing there?" I asked, a bit self-conscious.

"Oh, I came in a while ago, but you were still sleeping. I didn't want to wake you because you need to sleep."

By the look on his face, I knew what was to come.

"Could you talk a while?" he asked softly.

The last thing I wanted to do right now was talk. Yet, I heard myself saying yes. Pulling the chair closer to the bed, he sat down. I took a deep breath and held it. He was looking at me with such seriousness. I let out my breath slowly, waiting for the boom. Still looking at me, he reached out and took my hand. "How are you feeling today?" he asked, ever so softly.

"I will live," I said, trying to sound calm.

"You know, you gave us all a scare when you were out so long."

Hoping to change the subject, I asked, "Do others have this dengue?"

"Yes, quite a few of the others have it. This usually happens after a storm. As you have noticed, the wind is not blowing as much, and we have lots of water puddles. This usually breeds all kinds of mosquitoes."

I was getting really uncomfortable with him holding my hand. I could feel the heat starting again between our hands, and I tried to pull away but he didn't let go.

Suddenly, he said, "Tell me about Andy. Who is he? Is he the one you are running from?"

"Why do you want to know?" I asked.

"When you were in and out of consciousness, you kept calling for him. Are you afraid of him?"

"No! I am not afraid of him. He is my husband." With that, he let go of my hand and leaned back in the chair. His face was a mask of disappointment.

Trying to control his emotions, he said, "So you are still in love with him. That's why you were keeping me at arm's length."

"I tried to tell you," I said lamely, "that I couldn't get involved with anyone. I guess I didn't do a good job."

"I still don't quite know who I am," I continued in a pleading voice. "I have been so burned-out with doing everything everyone expected of me that I lost myself somewhere. When I left Boston almost three weeks ago, I never dreamed I would be in the middle of a storm. In spite of the storm going on in my life, I thought I could find the peace I was looking for here.

"After I came to the island of St. Ann's, I realized that too many people were there for my purpose. I needed to find a small island where I could hide, and no one would know me. I was here only two days when the storm came. This really threw me into a tailspin.

"I don't even know if Andy is aware that I'm gone. For all I know, he could still be too busy with his ministry to notice.

Andy and I have been in ministry for quite some time. At first it was fun. We went everywhere together. He is a pilot, and he made me feel secure to go on those long mission flights. We spent lots of time together.

"Things changed when he started to spend more and more time away from me. At first I didn't mind, then he was gone weeks at a time. We were going in different directions. I tried to get him to slow down, but he wouldn't hear of it. His TV and radio audiences needed him."

Doug was very quiet and sat staring at the ceiling. *What is he thinking?*

Just as I was about to speak again, he said, "Do you realize how similar our stories are?"

The pain in his voice almost brought tears to my eyes. He was such a sweet guy. I hadn't wanted to hurt him. When he spoke again, his voice was barely a whisper.

"You know, hearing your story made me realize how hard it must have been for Betty. No wonder she left."

"Betty?" I asked, knowing full well that she would be his wife.

"Yes," he said, "she was so full of life. I guess she died a little each day, not being able to cope when I left her alone with two small kids and was too tired to spend time with her. I remember now how hard she tried to get me to listen. 'You never listen to me,' she would say. She was right. My mind was always somewhere else."

The tears were running down his face now. "If I only knew what happened to her," he continued. "If only I had looked for her a little longer."

With his face buried in his hands, his voice broke with such pain.

Trying to comfort him, I said, "Maybe she lost her memory after she left and didn't remember who she was." He looked at me with bloodshot eyes.

Trying to control himself, he whispered, "Even if that is true, it's been twenty years since she left. She could have a new life by

115

now—another family. What hope do I have of ever seeing her again?"

"You never know. We can all hope. I think we have both helped each other. Seeing you like this makes me think that Andy might be worried about me. He is the type of person who will tear the Caribbean apart till he finds me. I know he loves me. He just got caught up with thinking that if he didn't do it, no one else could. Pastors and leaders find themselves so wrapped up in what they think they are doing for God that they sometimes miss the very thing God wants them to do."

"That is so true. It's not only in ministry, it's also with work. I drove my wife away with my work. Your husband drove you away with his church. When you look at it, we are not much different."

Getting to his feet, he said, "I don't think the Lord wants us to neglect our families and run around trying to save other families. It doesn't make sense. The Lord said we should love our families."

"So you do know the good Lord?" I asked.

"Yes, I grew up in the church. The members of my family are Christians. But when my wife left, I stayed away from the church."

"Why? Did you blame God for her leaving?"

"Yes, and even more when she didn't come back. I was angry with God for the longest time. Not knowing what happened to her was torture. I felt the least He could do was to let me know if she was dead or alive."

"You never know," I said. "God might not be finished with the whole matter yet. Are you still angry with Him?"

"No. I know that in order for me to survive this life, I must get to know His will for my life. I have since repented. That's why I do volunteer work whenever there is a need."

I noticed that his voice was no longer filled with pain. His spirit seemed lighter, almost as if a load had been lifted off his shoulders.

"You know, Deb, I was dreading this talk, but I am glad we had it."

"Me too," I said shyly. "If I were not in this bed, I would have found some way to avoid you."

"Yep, you have been running away from me like a wild rabbit. Now I know why."

We both laughed at that.

He stopped laughing and looked at me. "You do remind me of Betty," he said, "and if this Andy guy doesn't come get you soon, he will be in trouble." With that, he walked out the door.

I lay there thinking about how well our talk had gone. I had been so afraid of hurting him. I was right; he was still in love with his wife. *Thank you, Lord!* I prayed. *Please let him find out something about his wife, Betty.*

I started daydreaming about Andy. I realized how much I missed him. *Yet, can I trust myself to go back to the old life? Will it be any different? Can a man like Andy change after being wrapped up in stardom, with everyone telling him how great he is. If only he will take the time to listen. I know he will understand how I feel. He was so understanding when we met, so easy to talk to, so much fun to be with. Now it is as if he left and someone else took his place. I cannot understand how he changed so much.*

All of a sudden I felt the need to repent for being angry with God. I realized that God had nothing to do with the anger I felt toward Andy. I prayed again, *Please, Lord, forgive me.*

19

JANE

Jane turned the key in the lock, her mind a blur. *What,* she asked herself, *is going on with me?* She could not understand why she was having flashbacks from a recurring dream she had begun to have about three weeks ago.

She tried to remember the dream as she got out of her wet coat. As she thought about how cold it was outside, she remembered that her dream was about a beautiful island, warm with sunshine year around. She made herself a cup of tea and sat down to watch the news. Before turning on her TV, she looked around her small flat, thinking how warm and cozy it was. It was just enough for her; everything was within her reach.

Satisfied, she turned on the news. Suddenly, she sat upright in her chair. There in front of her was the island in her dreams. She could hardly believe her eyes. The newsman was saying something about a hurricane and described it as the worst storm to hit the islands in a century. Donations were being collected, and a phone number was given for people who wanted to help.

Things started coming back to her now. It was so long ago, but she remembered waking up in a hospital. She had been told that she was in a very bad accident. A car had apparently hit her, and the driver, thinking she was dead, robbed her and left her. An old couple found her when she was almost dead and brought her to the hospital. She was in a coma for months, and no one expected her to live. She had many broken bones, as well as torn tissues, and she needed to stay in the hospital for quite some time.

However, the old couple continued to come visit her. Since she had nothing to prove who she was, they assumed she was from one of the islands. She was known as Jane Doe. After many long, hard hours, she learned to walk and talk again. Over the years she had wondered who she was, but as time went by, she learned to live with whom she was now.

After leaving the hospital, she went to live with the old couple, George and Louise Anderson. They were kind to her and treated her like family, and she became Jane Anderson. They had no children, so they doted on her. George and Louise had been dead now for some time. Yet, Jane remembered them fondly, grateful that she was able to care for them when they got too old to take care of themselves.

In spite of all that had happened to her, she had a good life here in London. She was happy with her job at the hospital. Being a surgical nurse gave her the satisfaction of helping to bring healing and life to people in need. Yet lately, she felt as if something was missing. That's when she started having those dreams. It was as if she was caught in a trap and couldn't get out.

And now the island on the news was the same as the one in her dream. *What does it mean?* she wondered. *Can it be that I am from that island? But how did I get here to London? This doesn't make any sense,* she thought. Trying to put it out of her mind, she started to get ready for bed. As she walked into her bedroom, the phone rang.

It was Sue, her friend from work. "Jane, this is Sue."

"Hi, Sue, what are you doing calling this late?"

"I just had to call and tell you about the storm in the islands. It was a bad one. Did you see it on the news?" Trying to control her excitement, she continued, "We are all going to donate clothing and foodstuff."

"That's nice," Jane said, trying to sound calm. All this was too much for her. *I guess this is something Sue is used to, coming from Jamaica,* she thought. *If only I could remember something from my past, I would feel a lot better. But for now I must try to sleep; tomorrow is another day.*

She drifted off to sleep, only to be back in the dream again. This time she was lost on the island and couldn't find her way. She knew someone was looking for her, but she couldn't get to whoever it was. She was getting frustrated because she knew the island well. How could she be lost? It was like she was in a maze. No matter how hard she tried, she couldn't get out. She woke herself up, screaming and sweating.

Jumping out of bed, she splashed cold water on her face. Then she got back into bed, shaking with fear. *Dear Lord,* she prayed, *please take this fear away.* Lying back on her pillow, she tried to sleep again.

Jane woke to the ringing of the phone. "Jane," Sue shouted. "Are you still in bed? You're going to be late!"

"Oh, no," Jane said, half-asleep. "What time is it?"

"Late. You were needed in surgery an hour ago."

"Please cover for me, Sue. I will be there as soon as I can." All the way to work, Jane fought to get the dream out of her mind. No matter how hard she tried, she couldn't shake the feeling that the island she saw on the news was the one in her dream. She didn't have time to worry about it now. She had work to do.

Jane spent the rest of the day running and catching up after her late start. She breathed a sigh of relief when her break came. Just as she sat down to sip a cup of hot tea, Sue walked into the room with a bright smile, ready to chat. *Oh, no!* Jane thought. *This is the last thing I need right now.*

Sue, who was much younger than Jane, was so full of life. She seemed to have enough energy for two people. She immediately started talking and did not pay a bit of attention to Jane, who

121

was staring off into the distance. It took Sue a while to realize that Jane was not responding, and when she turned around to face her, she saw the tears streaming down her face.

"What's the matter, Jane?" she asked, concerned.

"I can't tell for sure, Sue. It's this recurring dream that keeps haunting my sleep. The island on the news last night is the one in my dream. I haven't been able to sleep much lately. It's been about three weeks since this dream started. I don't know what to make of it. Last night I had such a nightmare. I was lost on the island, and I couldn't find my way. I woke up screaming and afraid."

"So that's why you were late for work?"

"Yes. After I went back to sleep, I couldn't get up."

"Oh, you poor thing. I don't know what to think. Do you suppose this has something to do with your life many years ago? I remember you saying that you might be from one of the islands.

"Jane, you have to do something about this. A medical doctor from the islands named Douglas Davenport sent a letter to the hospital. It seems that they are running short on all their supplies. He was very convincing, and our hospital is getting together all it can spare. Why don't you send this doctor a letter and ask him to find out if you could be from this island. Explain to him what you have been told about yourself. He might be able to help you. You never know."

Though it was a long shot, Jane decided to give it a try. After all, what did she have to lose? If this would bring some peace of mind and stop the nightmares, she would welcome it.

"Great!" Sue said. "Then get some rest. I'll cover for you."

With that, Sue walked out the door. Jane leaned back in the chair. Pressing her fingers to her throbbing temples, she whispered a prayer. She closed her eyes and dozed off.

20

DOUG DECIDES TO FIND BETTY

Back at the shelter, Doug thought more about his talk with Deborah. What she had said made a lot of sense. He really hadn't looked very hard for Betty. All this time he had been angry with her for leaving. However, he had never given any thought to the fact that she might have tried to get back to him and somehow couldn't. What would it be like to see her again? He found himself thinking and wondering what she would look like.

Deborah was right. The fact that he had never married again could mean he was still in love with her. He realized what he was doing. He was building up hope that could hurt him. He couldn't go through that again. Yet he couldn't deny the strong feelings that had come to the surface when Deborah started talking about her life. He had tried to push those feelings aside for so long. He had told himself that it was no use thinking about something that couldn't happen. He couldn't take the risk of opening himself to be hurt again.

This was it for him. Whatever happened now, he would stay the way he was. Here he was a successful doctor, well established in his field. Yet he must admit there was something missing. It wasn't the Lord. He loved the Lord and spent many hours talking with Him. Most of their conversations were about his patients. He had never thought to ask about Betty because he thought she was happy with a family and didn't need him. He didn't think it was possible that she would want to come back to him.

Now, however, he felt a great need to ask the good Lord for help. *Lord,* he prayed, *if Betty is still alive, please let me know something about her. Even if she is happily married, Lord, I still need to know.* Feeling much better, he got to his feet and started to walk out of the shelter.

Debby

Things were starting to become a bit more normal on the island. The men were busy putting together some of the houses with boards they cut from fallen trees. The nails were no problem; they used the old ones. Everyone was excited as they waited for the arrival of the materials that would soon be coming from the main island.

I waited in bed for the bone-breaking fever to go away. After the third day, I was able to get up and walk a little inside the shelter. I was eager to go outside and tried to get to the door. However, that's as far as I got. I was too tired to go any farther and sat down on the nearest chair. Looking around, I noticed a considerable difference in the shelter. Almost all the injured were up and about, busy doing something.

I wondered where Mary was. Just then, she came walking in. "There you are. I was just coming to check on you. Are you hungry?"

"Is it lunch again?" I asked.

"No, child, you missed lunch. You was sleeping, so I didn't wake you. How about some soup?"

"OK," I said. "I am a bit hungry." I sat sipping my soup. It was good for a change. I could never figure out why everything tastes like medicine when one is sick. It must have something to do with the body. I heard somewhere that the body rejects food when it doesn't get enough exercise.

Sitting there with the sun hot on my face made me feel alive again. My mind went back to Doug. I hadn't seen him since our conversation. I wondered how he was doing. Though he was in good spirits when he left, I knew he had lots on his mind.

"How was your soup?" Mary broke into my thoughts.

"Oh, great! For the first time since this dengue, I was able to taste."

Mary laughed out loud, "That's a good sign that you are getting better."

"I still feel so weak. How long does it take for this thing to get out of your system?"

"It takes as long as it wants, child. But in a few more days, you'll be able to get around better," she said with a grin. "Now tell me," she continued. "Did you tell Doug about Andy?"

"Yeah," I said sadly. "He took it very well. At first he was very disappointed, even hurt. Then, as he listened to my story, he began to understand how his Betty felt. He blamed himself for not looking for her longer. And I was right. He is still in love with her. It would be so nice if he could find her. Wouldn't that be wonderful?" I said, excited for them to find each other now after so long. It would be just like God to show us He was working behind the scenes all along to bring about His plan.

Mary jumped to her feet, all excited. "I see," she said. "Sometimes God takes us out of where we are so we can see the storms that are going on in our lives. What a wonderful Lord," she continued, "to take the time to show us how much He loves us. We struggle so much with the little things that we miss the big things He has for us."

"So you are saying that we need to trust Him to bring about the changes in our lives."

"That is true, child. The good Lord knows what's best for us. He wants us to enjoy the fullness of His love, and we can only do that by trusting Him."

"This is great, Mary," I said. "If only I could remember all this when the world is crashing down on me."

"It's easy, child." she went on to say. "Just see yourself as a little child running to your daddy. Have you ever seen a daddy turn away from his child who falls down and calls to him for help? I have lived a long time, child, and I never seen it. Life is not fair. We will go through many storms, but the good Lord is fair. He will make a way."

I sat there looking at her. She was a simple lady and didn't ask for much. It didn't take much to make her happy. Yet her words burned deep into my spirit. She spoke with such wisdom and truth. I had never heard any thing like this before.

I felt a bit embarrassed for the way I had gone on about Andy and complained about not being appreciated. Although it was true, I should have found a way to make him understand. After all, he was just doing what he thought was right. Listening to Mary made me realize how much Andy sounded like her when we first met. He always said he had enough faith for both of us.

It seemed that she was reading my thoughts. "Don't worry none, child," she said. "The good Lord had a reason for bringing you to this island."

I looked up at her and smiled, "You know what, Mary? You are right." Reaching over, she gave me a big hug.

"You'll be a-right, child, you'll be a-right." We both turned around as Gus and Vera walked in.

"Hi, what are you two up to?" Gus asked, teasing.

"Oh, just shooting the breeze," I said.

"Good to see you sitting out here," Gus continued. "You have had your share of it. It seems that every time I look around, something is wrong with you."

"Well, Gus," I said, "I am just a city girl. I can't handle all this stuff!" With that, we all had a laugh.

21

GUS AND VERA

Debby

*G*us and Vera were spending* lots of time together these days.
Although no one said anything, it seemed that they were
becoming a couple. Usually little Princess would not be very
far from them. She was so beautiful. Vera was taking such good
care of her, and she looked to Gus as a father. *I wonder if she still
thinks about her mother.* I pushed the thought off, not wanting
to dwell on it.

I was beginning to get a sad feeling again. Leaving this island
would be very hard. With Mary and Joe, Gus and Vera, and little
Princess, I felt I had a family to come back to and visit. It would
be nice to see the work completed and the houses all put back
together. *Yet, with my situation the way it is, I don't know if I will
ever come back here.* The thought of never seeing this beautiful
place again made me shiver. However, I didn't have the energy to
worry about it now. *I should try to get back to bed and sleep a bit
before Doug comes and starts fussing.*

I started slowly to get to my feet. Feeling a little dizzy, I
held onto the back of the chair. I could not believe how weak

I felt. Just then Vera walked up.

"Need a hand?" she asked lightly.

"Yeah," I said. "Could you help me to the bed?" Taking me by the hand, she helped me walk to the bed. I was glad for the chance to visit with her. "Could you stay awhile?" I asked.

"OK," she said, pulling the chair close to the bed.

"How are you doing?" I asked.

After a brief silence, she said, "I am doing fine."

It seemed that she was having a difficult time talking about herself. "What is it, Vera?" I asked, noticing her nervousness.

She sat looking down at her hands. Then, looking up at me, she said, "It's Gus."

"What about him?" I asked.

"Well, he has feelings for me."

"What about you? How do you feel about him?"

"I don't know," she said. "I am still confused about all that has happened. I still miss my husband."

"I'm sure Gus understands how you feel," I said, trying to ease her mind, "and he can't expect you to forget so quickly. Try not to worry so much, Vera. It will all work out. Just give it some time."

"I think he is a good person, and I could grow to love him in time. But right now I can't think about getting involved with anyone."

"How do you feel about Princess?" I asked.

"I love her as my own daughter. I would love to take care of her, but we don't know if she has family on the big island. They, of course, would want to take her."

"What would you do, Vera? Would you stay on this island, or go to the big one?"

"I am thinking of going as soon as I can," she said without hesitation. "There is nothing here for me. All the rest of my family is back on the big island."

"What would you do there?"

"I have no idea right now. I need to be with my family, that's all."

128

I couldn't help noticing the sadness that had come back in her eyes. I felt responsible for causing her pain to come back. She looked away from me into the distance as the tears flowed down her face.

"Let it all out, Vera," I heard myself saying. "You will feel better after a good cry."

Wiping her eyes, she got up and walked out of the room. As I lay back on the lump I call my pillow, I thought, *that didn't go well. Poor Vera. She needs more time to adjust to the horrible experience of losing her husband and daughter.*

Still, I thank God for Gus. He is helping her get through the pain of her loss. If only he hadn't expressed his feelings for her so soon. It could have worked. I saw it coming, and I should have warned him. If I wasn't so wrapped up in my own problems, I could have had a talk with Gus. He is a smart guy. He would understand. On the other hand, he is young, and the young people today think they have to do everything right now. What a shame!

What will happen to little Princess now? Here I was playing matchmaker, not even considering poor Vera's pain. It's not even a month yet since the storm. She is still grieving for her loss, maybe still thinking that her little girl will show up. I cannot imagine how horrible it must be for her to carry all this pain. I was hoping that she was over most of it by now, but it's as fresh in her mind as if it were yesterday. As soon as I get out of this bed, I will try to spend some time with her. In the meantime, I will ask Mary to keep an eye on her.

I closed my eyes, thinking that I should try to sleep before it was time to have some of Mary's nasty bush tea. At least that's what I thought. Before I had time to entertain that thought, Mary was standing over me with that cup of tea.

"Oh . . . not again."

"Go ahead and drink it all up. You'll feel better before you know it."

"I will drink it for no other reason than to just get out of bed."

"That's a good girl," she said, smiling.

Taking the cup, I asked, "Have you talked with Vera lately?"

"No. Why?"

"She was very upset when she left me a while ago. I asked about her and Gus. She thinks Gus has feelings for her, and she is feeling pressured by him. She is still hurting from the loss of her husband, and not being able to find her child makes it worse. She is looking forward to going back to the big island to be with her family."

"Poor child," Mary said. "Can't say I blame her. She is so young and still has her whole life ahead of her. There is nothing here for her."

"What will happen to little Princess?" I asked. "Vera thinks she could have family on the big island, and they might want her."

"That would be great. I would like her to have a good home where she can be happy. She has gone through too much already in her young life."

"That is true, but she is young enough to forget and put all this behind her. Still I would like to see her once in a while. I intend to come back and visit when things are back to normal."

Mary smiled at that, "We would love to have you anytime."

"Thank you so much," I managed to say, thinking how nice it would be to visit with her. "How are things going with you and Joe?"

She looked up at me a twinkle in her eyes. "Well, we are talking about getting married, you know, doing it right."

"That's great!" I said. "When is the big day?"

"We want to wait a while till things get a bit more settled. That way we can have a nice place to live."

"Just remember," I teased, "you can't do this without me."

"Oh, I wouldn't think of it, child," she said with a big grin.

"I will be back later," she called over her shoulder as she walked out of the room. I lay there smiling, thinking of Joe and Mary together. How good they were for each other! Knowing they would have each other made me feel so good. At least, I wouldn't have to worry about either of them. For about the third time, I tried to close my eyes and get some sleep.

22

JANE
WRITES A LETTER

J*ane woke from her nap,* thinking about Sue's encouragement
to write a letter to the doctor she had seen on TV. With so
much on her mind, she had to act on this as soon as possible. *Is
it possible that this doctor might be able to help me learn my true
identity?* she wondered. *What is his name? Davenport! I remember
his last name. That's great!*

Getting to her feet, she buzzed around, finishing up the last
few minutes of her work. She grabbed her coat and rushed out
the door, thinking all the while how was she going to word the
letter. Stepping into her flat, she decided to wait a while before
turning on the news. She got her cup of tea and made something to eat. Then she sat down to see what was new on the
hurricane.

There it was again—the island. Suddenly she was back in her
dream. The flashback was so real it was like she was back there.
Shaking her head to clear her mind, she jumped to her feet.
"This is not good!" she said out loud, as she turned off the news.
She liked to watch the news, but now it had become a nightmare.

She decided to change the station and found an old movie.

Settling back in her chair, she tried to relax and forget the dreams. It was getting harder to concentrate on the movie. She closed her eyes, trying to block out the memory of last night, and felt sleep trying to take over. Getting up, she slowly made her way to the bedroom. Before she had completed her bedtime preparations, the phone rang.

"Jane!" Sue shouted at the other end of the line. "Did you get your letter ready?" Before Jane could say a word, Sue continued, "You have to get it in tomorrow. That's when we take the medical relief supplies in."

"So soon?" Jane tried to make an excuse that she didn't have time to write the letter.

Sue wouldn't hear of it. "Look, Jane, if you won't write the letter, I will!"

"OK, Sue. I will try to put something together."

"Please bring it with you in the morning."

With that Sue was gone, and Jane was left with the struggle of writing something about herself. She got some paper, sat down, and started to write. She couldn't believe how much she remembered. Before she knew it, she had written two pages. After looking over her letter, she finished getting ready for bed. She felt fear rising up from her nightmare last night. *How am I going to get any sleep if this continues?* As she crawled into bed, she whispered a prayer.

To her surprise, she woke fresh and well rested the next morning. With a big yawn and a stretch, she got out of bed. Feeling so refreshed gave her hope that she just might learn something about herself. As she stepped out into the cold air, she realized how alive she felt this morning, almost like the old Jane before the dreams started. Yet, the island in her dream did look warm and beautiful. She wouldn't mind one bit if she were from there.

Thinking about it now, she had always wanted to go to the islands for a visit. She had talked with Sue about going to Jamaica. They had discussed the beautiful beaches and the island food, as well as the spices. Jane was curious about why she loved the

23

THE
SUPPLY BOAT

Debby

I *woke from my nap to* find the shelter quiet. For a moment I didn't remember where I was. With my mind still in a fog, I tried sitting up. Then it all started coming back to me. I was in bed with this dengue!

"Is anyone here?" I called. No answer. I tried getting out of bed and found that I was still very weak. With great effort, I managed to pull myself to my feet. Looking around, I saw that I was all alone. Even the few injured were gone. *Well,* I thought, *it must be something big to get everyone out at the same time.*

It was a cool evening, and the sunset was breathtaking as usual. I was thinking how much I was going to miss all this. My thoughts went back to Andy. *What is he doing? Is he looking for me? It would be so nice to sit here with him and enjoy this sunset. He always said the best part of flying was enjoying the sunset. He would fly higher just to be in the middle of the beautiful rays of gold, yellow, pink, and all the other colors. Then after it had set, he would fly even higher to see it all over again.*

Deep into my daydreaming, I didn't notice the others

approaching. "Well, look who's up," Mary teased.

"Yeah, where did you all go?" I managed to get out.

"Well, child, the boat is back. It came in this afternoon while you were sleeping."

"That's great!" I said, a bit excited.

Just then Doug walked up. Smiling, he said, "Good to see you sitting up. How are you feeling?"

"A bit weak, but I'll live."

"I stopped by to check on you earlier, but you were sleeping. You need all the sleep you can get with this dengue. As Mary told you, the boat is back. I'll be leaving with it in a few days. Before I came here, I sent letters to some hospitals in the United States and England, asking for medical help. It seems we had a good response from both countries, and my presence is needed to meet with the medical boards. The supplies should be at St. Ann's in about a week."

I sat listening to him, thinking how excited he was. This was his whole life. He went on about having to go to the other islands to make sure they had enough medical supplies. I realized he was saying good-bye.

"So you won't be coming back," I said, looking away from him. I knew this was the right thing to do. Yet, I felt a sadness come over me at the thought of him leaving. Things wouldn't be the same around here without him.

Looking at me, he said softly, "I have to go. You remind me too much of her. I didn't realize it till you brought it up. You are right. I haven't gotten over her. I can't believe that I am still in love with her after all this time."

Trying to sound calm, I said, "With all my heart, I hope you find her."

"It would take a miracle," he said, "but our God is in the miracle business. And I hope Andy comes for you. If he doesn't, I will work my way back. There are a lot of things we need to work out."

"You would like Andy," I continued. "He is an easy guy to

be with. I hope you can meet him. You might even like flying with him. Who knows, with all that's going on in the islands right now, he could be thinking of flying again." Changing the subject, I asked, "How soon will you be leaving?"

"The boat might stay a bit longer this time because of all the supplies they brought. Some of the things will have to stay on board till we have a proper place to put them. First light tomorrow we plan to start building a storehouse for supplies. So we could be here for another two weeks maybe," he said with a grin.

"You know, things won't be the same around here without you." I said, looking at him.

"You could always come with me," he said teasing.

"You know I can't do that!"

"I know," he said laughing. He was still laughing when Mary walked up.

"You staying for dinner, Doug?" Mary asked.

"What are we having tonight?"

"Well, we have rice and veggies—and all kinds of thing we haven't had in a while," Mary said in her singsong voice.

"That sounds good," he said smiling. "I'll stay."

He turned back to me, rolling his eyes, still smiling. "I will miss her. She is always so happy; nothing seems to get her down."

"That's right," I agreed. "She has been a source of strength for me."

"Will you come back to visit after things are back to normal?" he asked suddenly.

"Yes, I would love to do just that. As a matter of fact, I plan to stay a bit longer on the big island when I leave here. To tell you the truth, I am not really looking forward to going back to Boston. This place is a paradise compared to Boston. I wouldn't mind at all if I could make this place my home and go back to Boston once in a while."

"Could you live here?" he asked, surprised.

"That wouldn't be a problem for me at all. It doesn't take much to make me happy. I will be fine as long as I have some food and water and a place to lay my head when night comes."

He was looking at me now with admiration, and I was getting embarrassed. *Not again,* I thought. *We've already been here. What is he thinking?* I was so relieved when Gus walked up.

Doug and Gus started talking about the building plans for the storehouse, and I sat listening to them. Doug was saying that more men had come to help. That would make sense. With all the supplies that were needed to rebuild this island, it would take many more people than we had here.

I noticed that the shelter was buzzing with new people, and it was then that I realized the boat was bigger this time. It had brought us plenty of food and water, as well as all the other things we had asked for. I was thankful for the sheets and pillow, as well as the fresh towels.

The more excited the others got about building, the sadder I became, knowing I would have to leave soon. The thought of leaving made me tired all over again. I tried to get to my feet, but my head was spinning. *What now?* I thought. *I guess I'm just hungry.* Looking over to where Mary was, I tried to get her attention. She was busy making dinner. Leaning my head back on the chair, I closed my eyes.

I must have dozed off. When I opened my eyes, Mary was standing in front of me, telling me it was time to eat.

"Could you help me to bed, please?" I asked. "I'm so tired all of a sudden."

"It's this dengue. It takes the strength out of you," she said. "Just rest now. I'll bring you some soup."

I was thankful for her strong hands as she tucked me in. She was gone but a moment before she came back with a steaming bowl of soup. "You drink up now. You need this to get your strength back."

Mary is right. I need to get my strength back. I slowly drank my soup, listening to the chatter in the outer hall. *How I hate being sick with this dengue!*

I woke to the noise of the workmen building the storehouse.

As usual, I knew I would be alone again. *I hate being in this bed.* *Today,* I told myself, *I will go outside, even if I have to crawl.* I was still thinking about this when Vera came into the room.

"Are you up?" she asked shyly.

"Trying," I said.

"Mary asked me to look in on you," she continued. "Would you like some eggs with bread?"

"Oh, yes," I said, "and some hot cocoa tea."

"You must be feeling better," she said, smiling.

"I am, and I will get out of this bed today."

"I don't know. Mary wouldn't like it. She is like an old mother hen. She kept watch over you and wouldn't let anyone come near you."

"That's my Mary—and you watch that old-mother-hen bit." I said teasing. Vera turned and walked away, smiling. She returned with my food, and it was so good to have eggs and bread. I ate as if I had not seen food in a long time. The fact of the matter is that my diet for several days had been only bush tea and broth.

Vera kept looking at me, smiling as I ate. "You look happy today, Vera," I said. "This is the most I've seen you smile."

"I had a long talk with Mary yesterday," she replied. "She helped me understand why I was so angry. I was angry with God for taking my husband away and also my baby."

"So she gave you a mother-hen talk."

"You could say that. I feel much better about myself now, and the thought of going home soon helps. You should see the boat. It's quite big, and they brought lots of stuff. The men are all working on a building to store supplies. Mary is getting supplies for lunch from the boat. That's why she asked me to come get your breakfast."

"Thank you so much, Vera. This was the best food I've had in a long time, and the cocoa tea was sooo good." Vera beamed as she walked out with the dishes.

Getting up was a lot easier today. I slowly got to my feet and made for the door. Yes, this was the day! Stepping outside, I heard the sound of hammering and banging everywhere. I thought I'd take it easy and not try to go too far. Just being outside made me feel better.

What a beautiful day it was! It looked like it was about mid-morning, the sun wasn't too hot, and there was a cool breeze. I started feeling like my old self again. Yet, I knew I must try to stay close to the shelter. Finding a shady spot under a tree, I sat down on a log. It was so nice to be out, leaning my head back on the tree trunk. I closed my eyes.

I was thinking about Andy again. I couldn't believe how much I missed him. *I hope he's taking care of himself. He never seems to eat right. I always had to remind him to eat. Anyway, he has Martha to keep an eye on him. Mary reminds me of her a bit. It's just like the Lord to put such caring people in our paths. He knew we were no good at taking care of ourselves.*

Sometimes the people of God are so busy that they run themselves into the ground. And when they are all broken up, they cry out to God to heal them. It has always boggled my mind why God in His wisdom would fix something so we could just break it again. I guess the good Lord, as Mary would say, loves us the way we are and puts up with us the way a father puts up with his children.

I thank God that he puts up with me because I am a mess. I can't imagine why anyone would want to be around me. Until Andy came along, I didn't think I would get involved with anyone. I felt I was too much of a mess to be part of someone else's life. Andy took me the way I was and never tried to change me. He always said, "I will not try to change you. You don't try to change me." We were happy with that. I felt that for the first time I had met a man I could respect. Now I don't know where he is and what he is doing. What went wrong? O Lord, we need help! I cried.

Maybe I had pushed Andy away. Maybe that's why he got so wrapped up in ministry. Did I try to change him without knowing it? He was the kind of man who could get along with anyone. He wanted to help everyone. He didn't like to see people hurt, especially

140

children and animals. I would tell him, "You can't save the whole world. God doesn't expect you too." He would laugh and say, "Yeah, but I can save a big chunk!" That's the way he was!

Before I had more time to think about Andy, Gus walked up and startled me.

"You were very far away," he said. "Where did you go this time?"

"Oh, I was thinking about my old life."

"Well," he teased, "you will be able to go back soon. Things are getting better here now, and we expect to have more people coming to help build. This island should be back to normal soon."

"Does this mean you will be staying?" I asked, surprised.

"Yeah," he said, rubbing his chin. "I am thinking about staying around a while."

"Tell me, Gus. Is something going on with you and Vera?"

"I don't know," he said, looking away. "I thought we might have something, but right now she's so far away. When she was injured, she was giving me the impression that we could have something together. I didn't pressure her into talking about us. I tried just to be there for her. I felt that she needed me.

"Now that she is better, I thought we might talk about a future together. The other day we went for a walk. We were doing well, and then I asked if we could talk about us. All of a sudden, she looked at me as if she was seeing me for the first time. She simply told me she was not interested in getting involved with anyone right now, that she was planning to go back to the big island as soon as possible. Then she turned and walked away from me."

"Oh Gus, I am so sorry. You seem to care very much for her, but you must remember that she is still mourning her dead husband, and she hasn't found her child. It's only been a little over three weeks since all this happened. She's really hurting a lot. You'll have to let her go. She needs time to get over the hurt and pain. You have been here for her, and she will remember how well you took care of her. Give her time to come back to you when she is ready."

"You are right as usual, Deb, but it's not going to be easy. She won't even talk to me now, and whenever I walk into the room, she finds a reason to leave."

"I think I know how she feels. I was there not too long ago."

"You mean with Doug?"

"Yes, but we are friends now. I have no reason to leave the room now, but he still makes me feel uncomfortable by the way he looks at me. It is just that I remind him of someone he loves."

"That must have been something—his wife leaving him like that, never to be seen again. That is not a good thing to happen on an island. No wonder he never got involved again." Gus continued, "I can't imagine how he got through it."

"With the help of God," I found myself saying.

"That's true, but sometimes it seems that the Lord takes his good old time to get around to doing things." Gus was serious now, as if he was suddenly remembering something he would rather forget.

I sat there looking at him. He turned to avoid my eyes, but not before I saw the pain in his. *What is he running from?* My thoughts went back to the fist time I asked him about himself. He had been so vague. It was obvious he hadn't wanted to talk about his life.

Clearing my throat to break the silence, I asked softly, "What is it that haunts you so and brings such pain to your eyes?"

Turning around to face me, still serious, Gus started to talk as if a dam had broken. Listening to him describe his life made me realize that the Lord truly had brought us together on this small island to stop running away and come face to face with ourselves. As a boy living on the island, Gus went to church with his parents. He loved the Lord and enjoyed going to Sunday school and reading the Bible stories of Jesus.

Then, when he was twelve, both his parents were killed in an accident. He was devastated, and, of course, he blamed God.

How could a God of love take his parents from him? Though everyone told him it was God's will, he couldn't see why God would want to hurt him. He was then sent to live with his grandparents. He was required to go to church with them, and he hated every minute of it. He decided that he wanted nothing more to do with God.

When He was older, he started to make plans to leave the island. After a few tries, he got a visa, and he was on his way to the United States. At eighteen, he felt that he had the world by its tail. He soon found out that being in New York wasn't all that he had expected. He was robbed and beaten a few times by people he had trusted.

He also met and fell in love with a beautiful girl, only to find out she was two-timing him and his best friend. He felt like a fool because he had planned to ask her to marry him. He was willing to forgive her, but she just laughed in his face and told him that she was not the marrying type. Being a simple guy from the islands, he couldn't handle this. He decided to come to the island to get his head back together. And that's how he found himself in the middle of the recent storm.

These past weeks, he had been struggling with questions about the reason God had allowed him to live. He remembered that after the storm he had asked God to help him find his grandmother and his cousins. Yet, after all his searching, he had found nothing. If he could only find their bodies, he would at least know what had happened to them. He had been full of anger and hatred toward them, and he wished now that he had not been so hard on them. They were only doing what they thought was best by trying to help him deal with his parents' death the only way they knew.

"So," I asked, after a pause, "Are you still mad at God?"

"No," he answered. "When I found myself alone, wet and cold after the storm, I was terrified. I thought I was the only one left, so I prayed and asked God to please let me find my grandmother. After searching all day and not finding anyone, I fell on my knees and repented of the way I blamed God for taking my parents and also the way I treated my grandmother. I rededicated my life to the Lord, and now I trust him with my life."

"That's wonderful, Gus," I managed to say, hardly able to contain the joy in my voice. "Mary is so right. She told me that the Lord brought all of us to this island so we could deal with the storms in our lives. You know, we sometimes don't understand the reason things happen the way they do. I have come to believe that God has a plan for each of us, and if we would trust Him, we could save ourselves lots of heartaches."

Gus was very quiet for such a long time that the silence between us was becoming uncomfortable. *What is he thinking?*

"To think that I spent all my teen years trying to get off this island," he said suddenly, "and now that I am back, I have found the girl of my dreams. It seems that I have gone full circle and come right back to find that what I was searching for was right here all along."

24

THE
LITTLE PRINCESS

Debby

Work on the storehouse progressed rapidly. Everyone was excited about placing the much-needed supplies in the storehouse. We were told that many more would be coming from the United States and England.

It was just about a month since the storm had come through, but it seemed much longer. So much had happened in the past month that I felt a bit older than my years. Again I wondered what Andy was doing. *Is he thinking about me?* Lately, that's all I seemed to think about. I was so wrapped up in my thoughts about Andy that I didn't see little Princess walking toward me.

"You not sick anymore?" she asked, shyly looking up at me.

Reaching down, I ruffled her hair fondly. "No, sweetie," I managed with a smile.

She went on in her child's voice, "You were so sick, and Miss Mary wouldn't let me come see you. I was so afraid that you would die like my mommy."

I stood there dumfounded. Her friend Sally, she continued, had told her that her mother was dead and was not coming back.

What can I say? She is so trusting, standing there looking at me as if waiting for an explanation.

With a lump in my throat, I reached down and took her hand. I managed to say in a shaky voice, "I'm so sorry you had to hear about it like this. We don't know for sure, but after all this time, we think your friend is right." I was surprised to see how well she took it.

Although she was still sad, she tried to be brave and said, "At first I missed my mommy, but I know she is with God. Sally lost her mommy too. And we will be best friends so we can take care of each other."

"That's good," I said smiling. "What about Miss Vera? You seem to be spending lots of time with her, and she takes good care of you. Would you want to live with her?"

"Yes," she said shyly. "She wants to take me to the big island with her."

"She had a little girl just like you, and her little girl is also dead. Miss Vera was very sad for a long time. Then she started to take care of you, and she is not sad anymore. You have brought joy into her life again. So you see, you can take care of her, too. You know, I will have to leave this island soon, but I will never forget you. You will always have a very special place in my heart. I will miss you so much," I said, reaching down and picking her up in my arms.

She giggled as I kissed her on the cheeks and put her back down. Running off with her friend Sally, she looked over her shoulder and said, "See you later!" Then she disappeared into the distance, her long, wavy hair blowing in the wind. *What a beautiful child she is! She's in good hands. Vera will take good care of her, and I know she will be well-loved.*

I was almost to the storehouse when I noticed Vera talking with Mary. They both looked up and waved as I approached. Not wanting to disturb them, I started toward the entrance. The building looked like it was almost finished. I guess enough people working together can build quite a lot in a few days. Inside, I was impressed with the amount of food and water, as well as the building materials the boat had brought. I walked out to find Vera waiting for me.

"Have a minute?" she asked.

"Why, yes. What's the matter?" I asked, concerned. "Is something wrong?"

"No," she said. "I just want to talk."

We walked off a little ways from the others and sat down on my favorite log.

"I had a long talk with Mary," she started, looking down at her hands. "I told her that I wanted to leave with the boat in a few days. She convinced me to stay a bit longer here until things are more stable. You see, I want to take Princess with me, and she felt it would be a bad idea to take her away from her friends now. She is also worried about you. After all, you are very fond of Princess, and Mary thinks you will be sad again if I take her away so soon."

I sat listening to Vera, thinking how sweet it was of Mary to be concerned about me. *But it's not about me.* I said out loud, "Princess would be better off with you. You have been taking such good care of her, and she loves you."

"Yes," Vera agreed, "she is very precious, and being with her helps heal the pain I feel from the loss of my own little girl."

"And you are filling the void she has from the loss of her mother. By the way, did you know her mother?"

"No," Vera said, thinking. "I remember seeing her around a few times. She was very sad. I had heard that she had lost the father of her child. I really don't know where she came from. Maybe Mary knows more about her."

"So that's why you told me the other day that she might have family on the big island."

"Yeah, something like that. I didn't want to get my hopes up and have to give her up."

"What has changed your mind?"

"It was Mary's talk. She helped me understand that by taking care of Princess, I was really helping myself."

"That's Mary," I said. "She is so full of wisdom. I really thank God for her. She has helped me understand a lot since I have been here.

"So, have you given any thought about you and Gus? You know he does care a lot for you, and he understands how you feel. You shouldn't shut him out. Just be friends for now, and then see what comes out of it. You said that in time you may grow to love him, so be his friend. I am sure he would be happy if you tell him that's all you want to be right now. He promised me he wouldn't pressure you. Have you told him you are planning to stay a bit longer?"

"Not yet, but I will."

"He loves Princess, and she adores him. She follows him around, and sometimes I see him carrying her on his back. I guess she never knew her father."

"Your guess might be right," Vera said, "because we never saw him."

"What about you, Deb?" Vera asked suddenly. "Will you be staying for a while?"

"I guess I have no more excuses to stay. As much as I would love to, I do have another life. Even now, my husband might be looking for me. The sad part is that he doesn't know where I am. But knowing Andy, he will not stop until he finds me."

"He must be quite a guy," Vera went on to say. "For a while there, we thought that you and Doug might have something going."

"Doug is a nice guy, and if things were different, we might. However, I am a married woman, and as soon as I told him about my husband, he understood. Besides, he is still in love with his wife, and he is hurting for her. My prayer is that someday they will find each other. Love is a beautiful thing. When two people find love, it should be forever. Being in love is the most wonderful thing in the world. This is the way God intended it to be."

Before we had more time to daydream about love, Mary joined us. "Come along," she said. "It's almost time for lunch."

Vera and Mary hurried back to the shelter to start lunch, while I lingered behind. Looking out at the ocean, I thought how nice it would be to have a swim. The water would be nice and warm at this time, but it was lunchtime. I started back slowly, not wanting to hurry and still feeling a bit tired. Hearing footsteps behind me, I turned around to see Gus running to catch up with me.

"Wait up, Deb," he said, smiling. "Where are you going in such a hurry?"

"Back to the shelter. Where else would I be going? I'm tired. This dengue left me worn out."

"Do you want me to carry you?" he asked, teasing.

"Don't tease me. I might just let you." We both burst out laughing.

After a while he said, "I saw you talking with Vera, and I was hoping to hear some good news."

"Well, you know, she won't be leaving with the boat in a few days, and she wants to be friends for now."

"That's good enough for me," he said, smiling.

"She will come around in time. Just be there for her, Gus, and you will win her heart. And please take care of Princess. She adores you."

"I know," he said, "and I love her as if she were my own. My hope is that Vera and I can get together and raise Princess. I will give her the time she needs to get over her loss. Then I plan to make a life together for us."

"Whatever you do, Gus, don't rush her. That is the fastest way to drive someone away from you."

We walked along in silence till we got to the shelter. People were coming in now, hungry and looking for food.

25

FLIGHT
TO LITTLE BRECK

Andy

The next thing I knew, I was being shaken.

"Wake up, Andy. We're burning sunlight."

"Sunlight? What time is it? It's dark outside."

"Yeah, it's almost four o'clock. We have to move."

"Who woke you up?"

"No one. I had some of that coffee. I haven't been to bed yet. The government received a radio message from the boat that left last week. Further down-island, there are two islands that have no runways and are in bad shape. Four weeks ago a small boat went there and left a doctor. The second, bigger boat arrived and called in a list of medicines. The government took almost five days to get it together. Then they called us. I understand the second boat has left."

"How far away are they? What are their names?" I was already up, and wide awake. "Let's go to the ready room and take a look at the chart."

"I already have, but you need to. Do you have any problem taking off without lights? The airport is closed."

"No, I can handle it."

We arrived at the ready room and poured over the charts. The islands were Little Breck and Unity. They were a couple hours away, with Little Breck being closer. I would stop there, unload what we had marked for them, and see if anyone had seen or heard of Debby. Then I would take off and go to Unity. I would try to get back to St. Ann's tonight. If we lost daylight, they would set truck lights at the end of the runway to guide me in. I would keep in communication by HF radio.

"Let's get the plane loaded," I spurted.

"All done. Did it last night while you slept, sleeping beauty," chuckled George, who was one of the ground crew and a mechanic.

I taxied onto the runway. The ground crew pulled a truck in behind me in case I had trouble after takeoff and needed to find the end of the runway to land again. I pushed the throttle all the way forward and started down the runway. The Caravan was heavy, fully loaded. I took off with no problem into the starry night, set my course, and settled down for a couple hours. I ate a ham-and-cheese sandwich and drank some strong coffee. I could understand why Jake didn't get to bed.

As the sun rose, I was again amazed at the awesome beauty of the islands—emerald in color—scattered in the blue sea below. It was breathtaking! I was captivated by splendor of God's creation when the warning buzzer on the GPS went off, telling me that I was approaching Little Breck.

It had been a beautiful small island, but was now devastated by the storm. As the plane approached, the people heard it and came out to see. I landed in a small, protected bay and taxied to a sandy beach. Jumping out onto a float, I threw a small anchor onto the beach.

At this point, the first people arrived. They cheered when I identified myself and told them my mission, and we started unloading the cargo. The men stood in the water and made a human chain. I took the relief supplies from the plane, and the men passed them to shore, where others took them to a nearby building. In less than an hour we had finished.

I was invited to breakfast. At first I declined. I didn't want to be a burden to them, and I had brought sandwiches with me. They insisted, however, and I joined them. While we ate fresh fruit and some of the sandwiches I shared with them, I showed them Debby's picture and asked if anyone had seen her.

At first no one recognized her. Then an older woman said she remembered seeing her on the boat. Debby had stayed on the boat and had gone further down-island. I asked where the boat usually went, trying to control my excitement. They said it depended on how much cargo it had for the other islands.

Now I was in a hurry to go, but they wanted me to stay. I finally explained that I had cargo with medicine for Unity, and they agreed that I should leave. They said Unity Island must have had it bad, too.

26

DOUG
RECEIVES A LETTER

Doug sat quietly, eating. He didn't notice all the chattering around him. He had just received a letter that had come in with the boat. For some reason, it had been misplaced when the others were delivered. He had read it, and for the first time, felt he had some hope. Yet, he couldn't bring himself to hope.

A woman named Jane was asking if he might know something about her. She had seen the news about the storm, and she worked at a hospital that responded to his letter for help. *Could this be Betty?* he thought. *I do believe that God is in the miracle business.* His mind was full of confusion. He had to stop thinking like this. He told himself he was hoping too much, too fast. Yet, deep down in his spirit, he knew that this could be something big. He knew that he had no way to get back to the island of St. Ann's, so he had to cool his heels here for the time being.

His mind drifted back to the day he came home and found Betty gone. *If this is her, how am I going to handle it if she has a family? She didn't give much information about herself— only that her name is Jane Anderson.* As much as he would love it to be her, he couldn't see how this woman in England could be her.

Betty knew no one in England. Why would she go there? Yet, did she go this far to get away from him? O God! he prayed. *Give me the strength to hold on until I know the truth.*

He felt a calmness come over him, and he knew that whatever came out of this, the Lord would give him the strength to handle it. After all, he had prayed and asked the Lord to let him learn something about Betty. Feeling better now, he remembered how many times the Lord had answered his prayers in the past.

He thought about the way he had been too proud and arrogant to ask the Lord for help in finding her. His pride and hurt had kept him wrapped up in his pain. He had pushed her out of his mind because she had the nerve to walk out on him, but he couldn't push her out of his heart. If she were happily married, then he would be free to let her go. At least, however, he would have the chance to ask her forgiveness for the way he treated her.

Debby

I looked over to the place where Doug was sitting with the other men and noticed that he was not paying a bit of attention to what was going on. His face was a mask of confusion. I wondered what had taken him so far away. Getting to my feet, I walked slowly across the room to where he sat.

"Are you OK?" I asked.

Shaking his head to help clear his mind, he asked, "How long have you been standing there?"

Without answering, I went on to say, "I saw you sitting here, staring blankly with such a troubled look in your eyes. I just had to come over to see what's going on with you." I was looking at him now with concern.

Pushing his plate away, he got to his feet like someone waking up from a dream. "Could you walk with me outside? I'll tell you all about it."

We walked a bit in silence. By the look on his face, I knew something was very wrong. A little ways from the shelter, Doug turned around suddenly and handed me the letter he had been reading over and over.

"This letter came with the boat, but I only got it this morning." I reached out a shaky hand, took the letter from him, and sat down to read.

Dear Dr. Davenport:

I am writing this letter to you with the hope that you might be able to help me find out who I am. My name is Jane Anderson. This name was given to me by the people who found me about twenty years ago. I was in an accident and was left to die. Since I was lying on the streets, I was robbed of all my personal belongings. When I was found by the Andersons, I was barely conscious. I was told that I might be from one of the islands. I saw the news about the hurricane. Since we are sending medical aid to you, I was wondering if you could give me any information that might help. I can't remember anything about living on an island.

Thank you,
Jane

I looked up at Doug, tears streaming down my face. "This could be her! Oh, Doug, could it be that the Lord has heard our prayers? We have all been praying. It would be so wonderful if this is she. I am so happy for you."

"Mary said the good Lord knows what He is doing," I continued. "He does everything in His own time. All we have to do is trust and believe that He is able to bring about His plans for our lives."

"This could be Betty," Doug agreed, "but she could be married and have a family. She didn't say anything about that. I won't build up hopes concerning us. It's been twenty years. She might not want anything to do with me, but I did ask the Lord to let me know what had happened to her."

"You must go to her, Doug. You must not waste any time. If this is her, you have to know right away!" I jumped to my feet with excitement.

"Yes, I know," he said, "but what if it isn't? I don't know if I can take another disappointment. Anyway, the boat won't leave for a few more days, and there is no other way out of here."

As we started back to join the others, I said again, "I'm so very happy for you. At least now you will find out what happened."

"One way or the other, I guess this will put an end to the questions in my mind," he said.

27

JANE DREAMS
OF HER ISLAND
IN THE SUN

*N*ow that the letter had gone, Jane was thinking that she had made a mistake in sending it. *What if this doctor thinks I'm some mad woman looking for sympathy?* she wondered. *Sue is all excited about it and won't stop talking about it. She keeps going on and on about this doctor.*

Weary from her day's work, she made her way to her flat. It was getting colder now, and Jane was thinking how much she needed a vacation from the cold. Stepping into her warm, comfortable flat with a sigh of relief, she decided a hot cup of tea was what she needed. With this in mind, she headed for her little stove. Settling in her favorite chair and sipping her tea, she was almost afraid to turn on the news. Taking a deep breath, she flicked on the TV.

There it was again—the island. The newsman said that things were getting better on the islands, and people were being helped in many ways. Help had come in from the United States, and churches were sending supplies that were being used throughout the islands. She sat with a lump in her throat, wondering why he didn't say anything about England.

Just when she was about to get all upset, the newsman said that medical supplies had been received from England. The news department was hoping to have an interview with the doctor who had requested the supplies. However, he was stranded on one of the smaller islands, and he wouldn't be back for a few more days. As soon as he was back on St. Ann's, he would be asked to give a report.

Jane let out her breath slowly. She didn't realize that she was sitting forward in her chair, hanging onto every word from the newsman. *It's done!* Jane thought, leaning back in the chair. *The doctor should receive my letter in a few days.*

Closing her eyes, she began thinking about the possibility of being from that island. Her mind went back to her dream. It was as if a small window had opened up in her mind, and it was confusing her. She still had flashbacks about it.

"Well, all this will have to wait," she said out loud, as she got ready for bed. Shivering as she pulled the covers over herself, she prayed again, *Dear Lord, please let me sleep in your peace so I will be rested to start another day afresh.* With that, she drifted off to sleep.

Again, she was on the island in her dream. This time she wasn't afraid. Everything was beautiful. The sun was out, and all the flowers were in bloom. In her dream, she was walking around, smiling and enjoying the sweet perfume of the flowers. Somehow, she felt like she belonged there. She was sitting in the sun, basking in its rays, when all of a sudden she heard a ringing in the distance.

Her alarm clock was telling her that it was time to get up. Jumping to her feet, she rushed to get ready for work. This was going to be a busy day, and she didn't want to be late. On the way to the hospital, her thoughts went back to her dream. How different it had been from the other times! She sat daydreaming about how wonderful it would be just to sit in the warm sun. Before she had more time to think, it was her bus stop. She breezed into the hospital, a smile on her face.

160

Sue met her as she walked in. "What happened to you? You look so different! You're smiling. Go on, tell me what happened!"

"Well," Jane replied, "I had another dream about the island last night. It was different; it wasn't a nightmare. I loved being there."

"Oh," Sue answered, "It sounds wonderful! You will have to tell me more during our break. Right now we have a full schedule." With that, Sue ran off.

Jane was left standing, staring at Sue's back. Humming as she turned to her stack of files, she decided to enjoy this beautiful day. She was well rested, and at this moment, she felt she could take on her heavy workload. In spite of what had happened the past few weeks, she now felt hope that there were answers to her questions.

28

DOUG
GOES TO ENGLAND

The storehouse finished and the boat unloaded, Doug made plans to go back to St. Ann's. He still found it hard to believe that he could find Betty after all this time. For the first time in years, he had found hope he thought he would never feel again. The boat was leaving the next day, and he planned to spend some time with Deborah. Somehow, he knew he might never see her again.

Stepping out into the sunlight, he felt at peace. There she was, smiling as she walked toward him, her dark hair flowing in the wind. He caught his breath, thinking how much she reminded him of Betty. As he stood looking at her, he thought, *how beautiful she is, so full of life! She looks like a beautiful flower, smiling in the sunlight. How could any man push her in a corner? Yet, I did that to Betty.*

He remembered how proud he was when people remarked on Betty's beauty. She was so happy to be with him and would wait up for him, even when he was called out in the middle of the night. He was so wrapped up in his work that he didn't notice how sad and quiet she had become. He made a promise to himself that if he found her, he would never let her out of his sight again.

Debby

I noticed that Doug was deep in thought. As I got closer, I didn't want to disturb him. He had that look on his face again.

Then he smiled and said, "I was coming to find you. I will be leaving with the boat in the morning, and I was hoping we could spend some time together." Seeing the look on my face, he continued, "I wanted to tell you about my plans to go to England and try to find this Jane."

"Oh, that's wonderful!" I said, smiling.

"I plan to leave for England in about a week. I might not see you again. By the time I get back to the island, you might be gone. I wanted to spend this time with you to thank you for helping me see what a fool I've been. If you hadn't come to visit, I might have gone on missing out on a great part of my life. You brought feelings to the surface that I thought were gone for good."

He paused and then continued. "I only pray that this Jane is my Betty. If she is happy and has a family, then I can move on and try to find some happiness. But if she is not married and is willing to take me back, I will spend the rest of my life trying to make it up to her."

We came to a shady spot and sat down. Doug stopped talking. He was looking out at the water, and I could tell he was hoping this Jane would be Betty. I prayed that she would be, for his sake. I couldn't bear the thought of having him go through all this for nothing. Reaching over I touched him gently on the shoulder. "Are you sure you want to go through with this?"

"Yes! I know it's a long shot, but I must find out. Don't you see, Deb?" he continued, "I must know for sure." Looking at me, he said, "What about you, Deb? What are you going to do if Andy doesn't come for you?"

"Oh, he will!" I said, trying to sound confident. "I will just wait here for him. If I know Andy, he is out there doing whatever it takes to find me."

I continued and told Doug how much he had helped me face

my own problems. "I felt like a little, lost girl when I came here, not sure of anything. I was so burned-out. Had it not been for you and Mary, I would not have made it. You are a wonderful person, Doug. I would be honored to continue to be your friend."

He smiled and said, "It would be nice if you and Andy could come visit sometime. He sounds like a great guy. I would like to meet him."

"We would love that. Maybe we'll stay awhile, and you can show us around your lovely St. Ann's." With that, we started back to join the others.

After dinner, Doug said his good-byes to us. We all shed many tears, as he had become one of us. In the morning, we all watched as the boat slowly disappeared over the horizon. Doug was on his way to England.

Doug fastened his seatbelt as the plane was coming in to land. He knew it would be cold here. It had been a long time since he had been in a cold country. The closer he got, the more he wondered if he done the right thing in coming. He had volunteered to come to England on behalf of the islands and thank the hospitals for their quick responses to his plea for help. He knew he didn't have to go, but he wanted to because of the letter.

The hospital was not expecting him until the next day, so he would have time to pull himself together. It had been a long flight and he was bone tired. He needed to have some dinner and a good night's sleep. His hotel was near the hospital, so he didn't have to wake up too early. He was sitting with his eyes closed, so wrapped up in his thoughts, that he didn't realize the airplane had come to a stop. He heard the stewardess asking, "Are you all right, sir?"

He opened his eyes, a bit embarrassed to find the plane almost empty and the stewardess looking at him with concern. "Oh, yeah, I'm fine," he managed to mumble, getting to his feet. He stumbled out into the cold night air, thinking how different this place was from his beautiful, warm island. Hailing a cab, he headed to his hotel. He had just enough time to grab a bite to eat before he succumbed to the weariness of the day.

As he got ready for bed, he wondered what surprises the new day would bring. His head had barely touched the pillow, and he was out like a light. He woke with a start, not remembering for a moment where he was. Then it all came back to him. He got out of bed, thinking, *this is the day*... The telephone cut into his thinking.

"Dr. Davenport?" The voice on the other end was very businesslike, but polite. "Welcome to England! My name is Don Wilson, and I am the hospital representative. We trust that your flight was pleasant and you had a good rest. We will be sending a car to pick you up at ten-thirty. Will this give you enough time to be ready?"

"Oh! What time is it now?"

"It's eight-thirty. We wanted to give you some time to rest."

"Thank you very much," Doug managed to say.

"OK then, Doctor. I will meet you in your hotel lobby at ten-thirty."

"I will be ready," Doug said and hung up. As he took an extra-long shower, he felt that things were working out better than he had expected. Taking one last look around the room to see if he had everything, he went to the restaurant for breakfast. He hadn't realized how hungry he was until he sat down and smelled the inviting aroma of coffee, different kinds of tea, and pastries. A young waitress took his order, and in a short time, he was enjoying his very hot coffee.

He started thinking again about the letter and the woman named Jane. All of a sudden, he felt a lump in his throat. *Could she be Betty?* He had asked himself this question over and again since he got the letter. *If this is Betty and she is happily married,*

I must find a way to face the facts. "Oh God," he prayed, "this is going to be so hard!"

Pulling himself together, he thought about his plans for the day. He knew he was to meet with the newspeople at the hospital and possibly with Jane. He decided to take care of his hospital and news commitments first and then try to find Jane. Before he knew it, Don was standing in front of him, extending his hand and smiling.

"You must be Dr. Davenport?"

After the formal greetings, Don asked, "Are you ready? We have a very full schedule ahead of us. Dr. Williams, our administrator, is a very busy man. He does things on a schedule."

Driving to the hospital, Doug turned to Don with a smile and said, "You can call me Doug." When they arrived, Doug noticed that the hospital was quite large, very much like the one in which he had done his internship. Doug was whisked into the administrator's office and exchanged the usual introductions and greetings. Then it was time for the news conference.

Doug felt a bit nervous as he stood in front of the news cameras, but he was used to public speaking and just plunged in. He started by thanking the hospital for its quick response to his letter. He went on to say that many people were helped, not only on the island of St. Ann's, but also on many other islands. Doug reported that many lives were lost and a large number of homes were destroyed. He explained that it would take a very long time to rebuild.

Sue and Jane were both busy with surgery that morning, so neither of them had seen Doug come in. Sue came out first to find the other nurses all glued to the TV. The handsome Dr. Douglas Davenport from the islands was giving a news conference. Sue stood looking at him, wide-eyed.

Then Jane walked in. "What's all the fuss?" she asked, without looking at the TV.

Sue grabbed her by the arm, turning her around toward the TV screen.

"It's the doctor from the island, Jane! He's here! Do you know what this means? You can't let him leave without seeing him."

Jane just stood looking at the face on the TV screen. Something deep within her started to stir. *What is this?* Suddenly, her heart began to race. She felt a bit faint. *What's happening to me?* she wondered. She had to sit down. Sue was looking at her with concern now.

"What is it, Jane?" she asked.

"I don't know, Sue. All of a sudden, I don't feel so good."

Sue got some tea and sat down next to Jane. The two sat in silence, sipping their tea. The news conference was over, and things were getting back to normal. Doug decided to hang around to see if he could catch up with Jane. Don had volunteered to show him around.

Stepping into the children's ward, deep in conversation with Don, he didn't see the two nurses standing in the far corner. Don was explaining the different kinds of medical problems as they walked along the ward.

Then Doug noticed the two nurses talking, going over a chart. The older one turned slightly, just enough for him to catch a glimpse of her profile. He stopped. Feeling the need to sit down, he reached for the closest chair. He felt that he couldn't take another step. *Could this be her? This must be Jane, but this is my Betty!*

Don kept on talking. He hadn't noticed that Doug was sitting. Doug was oblivious to Don. All he heard was a drone behind him. His heart was pounding, and his breath was coming in short pulses. He watched the nurses as they went about their duties. Without ever noticing him, they left by the other door.

Doug was still in a trance when he heard Don say, "Well, Doctor, did you get all that?"

"Oh...well, yes...um, I was feeling a little woozy."

"Are you all right? Would you like a cup of tea?"

"Well, yes! That would be very nice right now."

"Fine, there is a cafeteria right down the hall on this floor."

All Doug could think about was getting somewhere to sit and

collect his thoughts. *What do I do now? I thought that if it were she, I would just talk to her and settle it. Now I can't seem to move or think straight. After twenty years, what do I say... Hello, I'm your husband. Let's go home now... or... Hello! My name is Dr. Doug. No no! Too formal. Maybe... Hello, I'm Doc Doug from the islands. Remember you sent me a note? Yeah, that's better! Then what?*

"Do you want milk in your tea?"

"Um...what...Oh, no, just a little sugar, thanks." *OK, I'm that far...Yes, I know who you are...No, too quick...Please sit down.*"

"Well, Doctor, what do you think of our hospital?" interrupted Don.

"It's fantastic. If only we could have something like this on St. Ann's. I have dreamed of something maybe a little smaller but equal in excellence. The people of the Caribbean need a hospital like this."

"We are glad you think so. Our board has in mind to possibly do just that. Please understand that it is still in the embryo stage. However, I have been asked by the hospital to suggest that you come and discuss it with our board tomorrow if you are interested."

"What can I say? Well, of course! What time?"

"I will pick you up at nine. We must be prompt."

"Yes, I understand."

"Hold on, I'm being beeped. I have to make a phone call. I'll be back."

"No, that's OK. I'll find my way. I want to see London anyway."

"I have to go, OK? I'll see you tomorrow morning."

With that, Don Wilson left. Doug was really in a spin. *How could all this be happening so quick?* As he walked through the children's ward to leave, he was thinking, *How can I get a note to Betty...Jane?* Just as he was passing the nurse's station he saw the woman who had been with Betty. He went to the counter. "Hello, I'm Dr. Davenport from the Caribbean islands."

At first Sue caught her breath. Then, remembering to breathe, she said too quickly, "Yes, I know. I saw you on the telly. Can I help you?"

"Well, yes. The woman I saw you with in the ward—is she um...Jane Anderson?"

"Yes, that was Jane."

"Could you give her a note for me?"

"Of course, Doctor."

Doug wrote a note.

To Jane Anderson,

I received your letter, and I can shed some light on your situation. Please, can you meet me at my hotel restaurant for dinner at seven o'clock tonight?
I will explain.

Doug Davenport

He folded the note and gave it to Sue. "Thank you," he said and turned to leave the hospital.

Sue almost fell as she ran down the corridor to find Jane. Finally, after what seemed almost forever, she found her. Sue, out of breath, tried to speak, "Doctor... note... you..."

"Sue, slow down. Catch your breath. What doctor, what note?"

"*The* doctor, *this* note," shouted Sue, as she pushed the note into Jane's hand.

Jane found a chair and sat quietly as she read the note. Sue was beside herself with impatience.

"What did he say?"

Jane handed her the note. Sue read it and chirped, "I knew it. I told you. Wow! Are you going to go? Can I go too?"

Jane answered, "Yes, thank you for making me write the letter. Yes, I am going. And no, you can't."

"But I'm your best friend."

"Yes, you are and always will be...but I must do this myself."

"Oh, I guess you're right. But I sure would like to be there."

"Right now, I wish you could be there as me. I've waited twenty years for this. All these years of not knowing who I really am. Now I'm terrified. Could you come over and help me get ready? I need the moral support."

29

DOUG'S REUNION

Early that evening Doug was in his room, pacing the floor. He had started to get ready for his dinner date with Jane, but he couldn't decide how to dress. All he could think was what if she is married, what if…? It was getting close to six-thirty, and he had to get himself together. Finally, he decided to dress casual with a sports jacket.

She was still as beautiful as he remembered her. *What am I going to say?* he wondered. He decided to just wing it. No matter what he planned, it probably wouldn't happen that way. He left his room, took the elevator to the lobby, and turned right to the restaurant. He had made a reservation and was shown directly to his table. When the waiter asked if he wanted a drink, he replied, "No, just a glass of water."

His mind was wandering when he saw her being escorted to his table. He realized that his mouth was very dry, and he was glad he had the water. He stood as she arrived and was being seated. Then he sat down and extended his hand, saying, "I'm Dr. Davenport. You must be Jane."

"Yes. It's nice to meet you, Doctor," she said with a nervous smile.

She hasn't changed a day, he thought, as he looked directly into her eyes. An awkward silence followed.

Then she spoke. "Thank you for responding to my letter. In your note, you said you might have some information for me."

"Yes, I knew you before you left. You lived on the island of St. Ann's."

Jane, trying to control her emotions, leaned forward in her chair. She did not want to miss a word. Finally, she had met someone who could tell her about herself.

"Would you like to order dinner now? Would you like something to drink?"

"Well, yes, I guess so. I would like a cup of tea. Thank you."

The waiter took the order and brought the tea. They continued on.

"You were saying, Doctor?"

"Just call me Doug. Your name is Elizabeth. Everyone called you Betty." He stopped for a moment to let it all sink in.

She was thinking that there was something very familiar about him. Yet, she couldn't put her finger on it. He was so polite and respectful to her that it overwhelmed her. Then she asked him, "Do I have any family back in St. Ann's?"

Leaning forward and taking her hand, he said, "Yes, you have two children. They are grown now. I have pictures of them." Without thinking, he added, "Your son is in New England, studying to be a doctor, and your daughter is studying law."

"You said you have pictures?"

He whipped out his wallet, opened it to two pictures, and gave it to her. She sat staring at the pictures, thinking how much the girl resembled herself. She caught her breath as she realized that her son looked like the doctor sitting across from her. She lifted her head slowly, and their eyes met.

"Yes, I am their father."

With tears streaming down her face, she responded in a voice that was barely a whisper, "Then you and I?"

"Yes, you and I were married twenty-five years ago. I came

home one day, and you were gone. You disappeared without a trace. We searched for you, but never thought of looking in England." He was looking deep into her eyes as she sat and wept quietly. He wanted so much to hold her in his arms and tell her it would be OK.

She burst out suddenly, "Oh! If only I could remember what happened? All I know is what I have been told by the Andersons. How could I have left the island and ended up here?"

"And my children?" she asked. "Who took care of them?" She was looking at him now with pleading eyes. Before he had a chance to respond, she continued, "What did you tell them happened to me?"

"I had no choice but to tell you were dead."

She felt like her heart had just been ripped out of her chest. "How...how..." she gasped, "did they take it?"

Not wanting to cause her more pain, he tried not to go into much detail. "They missed you. They were very young. They thought you were with Jesus, and they would get to see you again." She was weeping uncontrollably now, and his heart was breaking. He wanted so much to comfort her. He was about to get up.

"Who gets the curried chicken?" the waiter broke in.

After the dinner was served, she sat wiping her eyes, "I'm sorry."

He responded, "For what? I am the one who caused you to run away. I was so wrapped up in my work, and you were left alone with the children. You tried to tell me how lonely you were, but I was too busy to listen. Can you forgive me? I am truly sorry for all the pain I have caused you."

They sat in silence for a while. Neither of them had touched their food. Doug continued, "I understand that all of this is very sudden. But there is something I need to know." Holding his breath, he asked the question that was heaviest on his heart. "Are you married? Do you have family here?"

Her answer seemed to take forever. Doug didn't realize that he was still holding his breath.

She answered, "No—to both questions."

He exhaled slowly. *Thank God,* he thought.

She continued, "I never felt the need to get involved with anyone. After my accident and my long stay in the hospital, I went to school to become a nurse."

"You were already a nurse," he burst out.

"That answers some questions. It seemed that I had always been a nurse."

"It's getting late. We still have many things to talk about," he said.

"How long are you staying," she asked.

"It really depends on you. I have wanted to find you for twenty years. I never stopped loving you. I am here until we decide what we are going to do."

"What about you? Did you ever get married again?"

With a look of tenderness in his eyes, he said, "After you left, I spent so much time looking for you. When I couldn't find you, I buried myself in my work. I never had the time to think about it. Besides I couldn't find anyone to take that special place you held in my heart."

Looking at this handsome man, she wondered how she could have walked out on him. She asked shyly, "Does this mean there is still a chance for us?"

He could hardly believe his ears. She had asked the question that expressed his heart's desire. "If you would have me, my dear, I will spend the rest of my life making it up to you." He continued, "I know it will take some time, but I would like to try to help you remember your past."

"I would like that very much," she whispered with a faint smile.

He was excited. Taking her hand and looking deeply into her eyes, he said, "As soon as I am finished here, we can go back to St. Ann's together. We could take it slow, get to know each other again."

"Oh, Doug! That would be wonderful!"

With that, he reached over and kissed her gently on the lips. She felt like a schoolgirl who had been kissed for the first time. This was the beginning of the long road back.

30

LANDING
AT UNITY ISLAND

Andy

I took off from Little Breck with my heart pounding. I waved my wings to say good-bye and set my course for Unity. Forty minutes later, the GPS was beeping. I was close. I could see it clearly. Even with all its devastation, it was still a beautiful island. It had a protected beach and a few buildings were standing. They looked as if they had been repaired, and a newer building was to one side. I gracefully kissed the water, and the bird set down. My heart was pounding, *Is Debby here?*

I knew I was on the right track. I had radioed to Jake about my landing at Little Breck and my delivery of the relief supplies there. He had given me the green light to use my own discretion, but to keep him informed. Of course, I was limited to my fuel supply. Finding jet fuel on a little Caribbean island was highly improbable.

I taxied up to the beach and shut down. I tossed my little anchor on the beach as usual. The people came running down the gentle slope to the plane, but I didn't see any sign of Debby. I opened up the plane, and the men formed the usual human chain in the water. We quickly unloaded the cargo, and I jumped to the beach and brushed myself off. Now I could start to ask about Debby. I wondered if anyone had seen her here. My heart started to pound.

Debby

I found myself thinking about Andy. *What is he doing? Is he trying to find me?* I was so deep into my daydreaming that I didn't hear the plane come in. All of a sudden, Mary burst into the shelter shouting.

"An airplane just landed on the water."

I jumped to my feet. It was Andy. He was the only one who would be crazy enough to do a thing like that. After all this time talking about him—now that he was here—I was a nervous wreck. Trembling, I looked at Mary and said, "You go and see if it's really him."

Mary responded by saying, "You know it's him, child. Pull yourself together. The good Lord has brought him to you. It's your Andy all right. You knew he wouldn't stop till he found you." Starting out the door, she looked back over her shoulder and said, "The others are already at the water's edge, helping to unload the plane."

I whispered a prayer of thanks and started for the door. As I stood in the doorway, I stared at the man coming up the path. He looked like Andy, but there was something different about him. He had a beard and his clothing was not the type he had worn these past years. I felt myself becoming weak in the knees and held onto the doorframe for support. Mary, standing next to me, reached her arm around my tiny waist to keep me from sliding to the floor.

He showed the picture to the men closest to me. They all pointed Andy toward the shelter with big grins on their faces. All of them realized that this was the Andy they had heard about.

Andy

I looked toward the shelter, and at first all I could see was two women standing in the doorway. The sunlight was in my eyes. Then I realized the smaller, younger one was Debby. I didn't know what to do. I tried to move forward, but my legs didn't seem to obey me. My mind exploded, "It's Debby! I've found her. She's OK!"

I started up the path, my feet feeling as if they weighed a hundred pounds each. It seemed to take me hours to cross the slope to the shelter. As I came near, I could see a nervous smile on her face. "Debby! I'm here!" I shouted.

Mary broke into laughter and stepped out of the way. As she moved, she let Debby go. Debby started to sag slowly down the doorpost. I reached out and caught her in my arms. At the same time, as a reflex, she threw her arms around my neck.

There was a cheer from the beach, and Mary stood weeping with joy. As I held Debby and felt her softness and warmth, I recognized her familiar smell. My mind was on a single track. All I could do was repeat over and over, "Debby, I love you, I love you, I love you."

Debby just held on tighter and quietly wept. "I love you too," she sighed.

After what seemed like hours but was really only minutes, we leaned back without letting go and looked at each other.

I blurted out, "Are you OK?"

She just looked at me and without a word, nodded her head yes.

"Debby, please forgive me. Things will be different, I promise."

"I have been looking for you since the hurricane struck," I stammered. "Oh, thank God, I found you, and you are OK!"

Have You Been There?

This story is told as fiction, but it is based on true facts. The names and places were changed to protect the privacy of those mentioned. In trying to do the Lord's work, we sometimes find ourselves wrapped up in doing what we think He wants us to do. We hardly take the time to stop and ask Him what He wants. Sometimes we find ourselves burned-out from doing good works for God.

Have you been burned-out, lost, lonely, sad, cold, hurting, afraid of an uncertain future? Have you been so very tired that you just wanted someone to reach out and hold you and tell you that everything will be all right?

Well, there is Someone who is always there when you come to the end of your resources! You may think you can't go on! However, He is waiting to reach down and pick you up, to hold you close so you can rest your head on His shoulder.

This Someone is Jesus! He knows; He sees; He understands. He wants to heal your wounds, wipe away your tears, and take away your pain. He is the only One who is able to put the broken pieces of your life back together.

The choice, of course, is yours. You can turn and walk away, or you can reach out and take His hand. If you make the decision to take His hand, your life will never be the same.

About the Authors

Captain Charles and Rica Basel have been missionaries in the Caribbean for over twenty years. They are the founders and directors of the Salvation Navy of the Caribbean, Inc., a ministry God is using to change the lives of people from all walks of life. Their hearts and home have always been open to anyone in need—people who have been turned away by churches and find themselves facing homelessness or struggles with substance abuse.

They have traveled extensively throughout the Caribbean islands, bringing supplies and ministering to the forgotten people of the Caribbean. In recent years, their mission has taken them to the United States as an apostolic team. They have been through burnout and know others who have also struggled with it. They believe that this book will help others to understand that they are not alone. It is never too late to discover that God is bigger than anything we think we can do for Him. It is truly all about Him.

Captain Buck and Rica, as they are known in the Caribbean, live on the island of Puerto Rico. Captain Buck is a commercial pilot and also holds a United States Coast Guard merchant marine captain's license. Rica is a native of the island of Grenada and was educated in Boston. They have been married for twenty-three years, and they have five children and ten grandchildren.

To Contact the Author

E-mail: captbuck@coqui.net
Website: www.ourcaribbeanstories.com